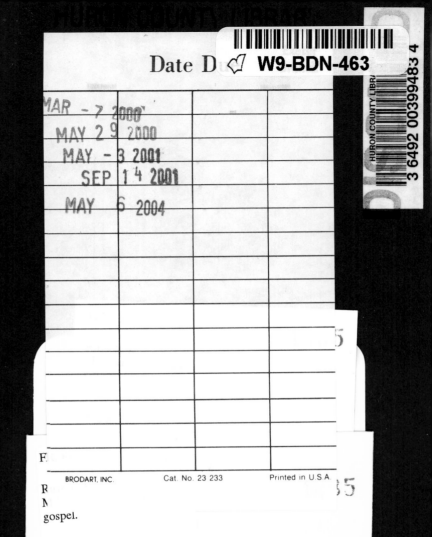

F.

R
N
gospel.

PRICE: $34.95 (3559/ex)

Mike and Gaby's Space Gospel

A NOVEL

KEN RUSSELL

LITTLE, BROWN AND COMPANY

A *Little, Brown* Book

First published in Great Britain by
Little, Brown and Company 1999

A CIP catalogue record for this book
is available from the British Library.

ISBN 0 316 85049 7

Typeset in Dante by M Rules
Printed and bound in Great Britain by
Clays Ltd, St Ives plc

Little, Brown and Company (UK)
Brettenham House
Lancaster Place
London WC2E 7EN

Dedicated to
The Rev. Gene Phillips, S.J.

Contents

I   UFO Over Eden 1

II   Godawful 11

III   Holy Intercourse 24

IV   Virgin Birth at the Holy Day Inn 35

V   Star Quality 45

VI   Hi-Jinks Over Jordan 56

VII   Enter S.A.T.A.N. 63

VIII   Is It a Bird? Is It a Plane? 69

IX   Dinner at the King David 84

X   Stoned 91

XI   Miracle in the Cat House 97

XII   Judas' Bag 106

XIII   At the Pax Romano Pizza Parlour 113

XIV   The Stiff Takes a Stroll 119

XV   Women!   131

XVI   Lox 'n' Bagels for Five Thousand 138

XVII   Running on Water 146

XVIII Palm Power 152

XIX   No Picnic! 162

XX   Scum in a Turkish Bath 170

XXI   The Last Cuppa   174

XXII   Sharon and Debby Point the Finger 181

XXIII The Little Ball-Breaker 185

XXIV   Rub-a-Dub Dub, Pilate's in the Tub 189

XXV   Crucifixion Carnival 194

XXVI   The Big Bang! 197

XXVII Oops! 202

Mike and Gaby's
Space Gospel

CHAPTER I

UFO Over Eden

inosaurs were a dead loss – twenty-five tons of solid stupidity.'

'Twenty-five million years of evolution and they still fouled their nests – up to the last fart!'

'Well, you know the old saying – "Happy as a dinosaur on a dung heap".'

'A dung beetle has more sense in its little finger.'

'A dung beetle, ah, *now* you're talking – now there's an evolutionary miracle. Given time it could invent the wheel.'

'Time is what we can't afford. We need a fast developer.'

'Like the blue-assed baboon, you mean?'

'Pity it developed a complex about its butt – could have gone far.'

'Imagine how far it would have gone in a skirt or a pair of shorts.'

'It might have got to Mars.'

'Or at least the moon.'

'I wonder how far these guys will get?'

. . . And the two-person crew of spaceship A.R.K. 2001 turn their attention from the controls to study a transparent cylinder in the centre of a cabin which owes more to Jules Verne than Cape Canaveral.

Lying in the cylinder side by side are a young man and a young woman. Prototypes of perfect human specimens. They are life-sized Ken and Barbie with the addition of penis, balls and breasts with nipples, not to mention the hint of a vagina.

So much for the cargo; what of the pilot and navigator? Well, if you can call to mind the robots of *Star Wars* then you have a pretty good idea. In the movie the tall gold one was called See Threepio and shorty, the blue and white one, was known as Artoo Detoo. But *our* metal friends are called Gaby and Mike and are a good deal more human (as *we* understand the word) in their behaviour than their Hollywood counterparts, and just a little bit fatter – in fact, Mike has something of a beer belly and Gaby is decidedly busty. The explanation for these Robotic similarities is simple and can be summed up in two words – racial memory. For the new species about to be consigned to space-lab Earth is soon to catch a glimpse of the two members of the race of Robots that created them. And once seen, never forgotten.

The Robots stare at the inert human forms with eyes switched to a modal mix of curiosity and compassion. For after a journey of twenty-five light years they have grown quite fond of the dormant couple, and have named them after two household pets of their acquaintance – a pair of Triffids called Adam and Eve.

For in these experimental prototypes the entire Robot Cosmos has placed its hope of survival. Having developed their own technology to maximum potential, they are still unable to find an antidote to the deadly virus which could eventually wipe them out. And in *Homo sapiens* – the creature with the biggest brain they had ever created and with an unprecedented capacity to learn and develop – they saw a creature that would eventually come up with a solution. At least, that was their hope. It had always been their hope – ever since the Earth had cooled down sufficiently to support life.

'They look pretty frail. Do you think they'll survive?' asked Gaby.

'They're programmed to survive,' replied Mike, 'providing they have the will-power, that is. That's a tricky commodity to programme.'

Their reverie was suddenly broken by the ringing of an alarm bell and a commanding voice on the PA system: 'Defreeze and prepare for landing, defreeze and prepare for landing.'

'All right, all right,' muttered Mike. 'We're not deaf.'

'And we're not dumb, either,' added Gaby, backing him up.

They pushed buttons, flicked switches – and as the liquid hydrogen was evacuated from their see-through cylinder, Adam and Eve started to breathe.

'Subjects activated,' said Gaby to the intercom.

'Touchdown,' said Mike.

And thus were the seeds sown for the greatest show on Earth.

Twelve hours after touchdown, Adam had his first hard-on. For though it was warm in Eden by day it was bitingly cold by night. Eden, by the way, was situated more or less where the Tel Aviv Hilton stands today. And as everyone who has been on the beach there at night knows, unless you're engaged in a little nooky you could wake up with a severe case of rigor mortis. So the young couple huddled together for warmth and the inevitable happened. Nine months later Cain was born.

In the interim, the first folk on Earth learned to survive. They found that the skins of dead animals could also keep them warm and that fresh water tasted better than salt water, that it was better to walk on grass than gravel and better to live in a tree than on the beach, and that it was nearly as much fun playing with yourself as playing with your partner. Life was good. Life was sweet. And when they got tired of picking fruit, they could always pick their noses. There was always something to do . . . should they ever feel so inclined.

'At this rate,' said Mike to Gaby in A.R.K. 2001, 'they're never going to get the wheel invented.'

'Maybe we should give them a clue,' suggested Gaby.

'Like dropping a coconut on their heads?' said Mike dismissively. 'You know we're not allowed to intervene in any way. That's the law! It would be contravening orders.'

'Maybe we should have located them somewhere less relaxing – in the northern hemisphere,' replied Gaby, 'a place where it's not only cold by night but cold by day as well and it pours with rain twenty-four hours a day, every day of the year.'

'You mean like there,' said Mike, stabbing a spot on the world weather chart that in Roman times would be known as Mancunia.

'They'd never make it through the first winter,' prophesied Gaby.

'What's that?' said Mike, suddenly moving to the scanner covering Eden. Gaby joined him at the monitor where a flashing light making *bleep, bleep* noises was fast approaching the spot where Adam was picking fleas from Eve's armpits and Cain was eating his own ka-ka and playing with a pet piglet. Open-mouthed, the Robots zoomed in for a closer look.

'Bugger me,' exclaimed Gaby, 'it's a ruddy Robot.'

'But not one of ours,' observed Mike with a note of disparagement in his voice, for like Gaby he was proud of his R.U.R. lineage. Rossum's Universal Robots were something special in the Universe in those early days.

'Flash up the Alien Identikit print-outs,' urged Mike.

'Check,' said Gaby, and a moment later a succession of images flashed up of every known alien mechanoid in the galaxy. But although there were some pretty weird shapes on display, this type was not among them. True, it stood on two legs and had two arms like most R.U.R. models but instead of metal it seemed to be encased in black plastic – rather like the humble dung beetle. In fact, its glossy features resembled a dung beetle even down to the big shiny eyes and the two antennae-like horns protruding from the top of its head. And there the similarity ended. For it also had a long swishing tail with a sharp, poisonous-looking barb on the end.

For once in their lives our friendly space-folk were speechless.

And so are Adam and Eve – but for a different reason: so far they've only learned to grunt – one grunt for 'no', two grunts for 'maybe'.

Then, without warning, the black intruder scoops up the piglet and slashes its throat with a knife that appears from nowhere. Blood splatters over baby Cain who starts to howl. Then the intruder tosses the piglet to Eve who catches it on impulse, only to let it go on realising it is dead. Seeing the blood on her hand, she licks it off. Pow! Something blows her mind and she looks at the piglet with a glint of sudden awareness in her eyes. This instantly sets her apart from Adam who is looking on with little curiosity or understanding. Snatching up the piglet, Eve begins to tear away at its flesh with her sharp teeth. She loves it, tosses Adam a piece of tender underbelly. His curiosity finally aroused, he follows Eve's lead and like her is imbued

with fresh awareness. A new intelligence appears to
dawn on him.

A fact that does not go unnoticed by the two technological miracles in the spaceship.

'You know something, Gaby,' mused Mike, 'here's a
guy who's gonna invent the wheel someday.'

'And just wait till he tastes roast pork,' replied Gaby.

'With hot apple sauce. That'll be the day,' said Mike.
'There'll be no stopping him.'

'The sky's the limit,' dreamed Gaby. 'And do you
know something . . . ' The thought dies on her enam-
elled lips as she watches the monitor.

The space intruder tosses the bloodstained knife at
Adam's feet and then points with claw-like hand at baby
Cain, who has lapsed into silence. Adam looks at the
baby and all that succulent flesh, far more tender than
that of the bristly piglet – and snatches up the knife. Eve
reads his mind and grabs hold of baby Cain, clutching
him protectively to her breast. Adam hesitates, frus-
trated. For a moment it seems that he will tear baby Cain
from her arms, whereupon Eve grips the baby, who has
begun to howl again, even tighter and gives one grunt for
'no'. Angered at being thwarted, Adam leaps to his feet
and vents his frustration on an unsuspecting sheep grazing nearby. Again and again the lethal blade rises and falls
with great ferocity till long after the animal is dead – and
Adam is exhausted. An apple falls into Eve's lap. She
takes a bite, licks her lips – and looks at Adam provoca-
tively. He begins to get an erection. She tosses him the

apple. Roughly, he takes a bite and, thoroughly turned on, pulls her towards him. A moment later Eve has gone down on him and they are heavily into oral sex.

'If this catches on the propagation of the human race is gonna be a slow process,' remarked Mike sadly.

'I never knew an apple was an aphrodisiac before,' mused Gaby.

'Not to a Barbary ape it's not,' said Mike. 'Seems this breed of monkey is more sophisticated.'

'Hey, look at the alien, he's blown his top,' exclaimed Gaby.

And sure enough he has. Steam is jetting out of the safety valve on the alien's horny cranium – with an undulating whistle, a whistle that in the 20th century would paradoxically become known as a 'wolf-whistle'. Then, as it reaches a shrill crescendo, the intruder vanishes – mission accomplished! A split second later Adam ejaculates and . . . KERPOW! There's a crack of thunder like the crack of doom. Even Mike and Gaby blink their little metal eyelids. Eve nearly chokes! Baby Cain shits himself and Adam doesn't know if he's coming or going till another clap has him taking off like Linford Christie jumping the gun and almost swimming through the ensuing cloudburst. And, grabbing the baby in panic, Eve takes off a split second after him.

Up in the spaceship where it is nice and dry the two Guardian Angels, for that is to be the destiny of these R.U.R. scientists, shake their tin heads and tut! tut!

'That woman's an animal!' exclaimed Mike.

'And the man's a wimp,' replied Gaby.

'And the alien, what do you make of him?' asked Mike, his metal forehead creasing into a frown.

'Stop that or you'll give yourself metal fatigue,' snapped Gaby.

'Do I take it that you have not computerised an opinion as yet?' said Mike.

'Well, I computed he's up to no good,' replied Gaby sharply.

'He's taught them to go against their natures. Man was not made to eat meat,' said Mike loftily.

'Really,' said Gaby. 'Then what about those two sharp teeth on either side of their mouths?'

'They're for things with thick skins.'

'Like you, for instance?'

'Like avocados and coconuts,' flustered Mike.

'You've got a thing about coconuts,' retorted Gaby, somewhat piqued.

'Where does that guy think he's going?' said Mike, changing the subject.

'Away from the thunder, I guess,' said Gaby, mollified once more.

'No way can he escape the thunder,' replied Mike. 'He's in for a big surprise.'

'He'll learn,' said Gaby flatly.

'Let's hope so, for our sakes,' said Mike, his feelings mode switching to 'caring'.

'Such rain,' said Gaby, her thought mode flicking between 'confusion' and 'contentment'.

'At least it's washing the baby's poop off poor Eve,'

said Mike, his work mode switching to 'playful'.

'What now?' asked Gaby, her duty mode overriding all others.

'We'd better report the presence of that alien force,' said Mike, clicking into the same mode.

'Do you think it'll hang around?' asked Gaby.

'Too bad we can't hang around to find out,' replied Mike, 'or we're going to be late for our date with Venus.'

'And she *always* gets top priority,' said Gaby, rolling her eyeballs.

'Have you launched the Eden satellite yet?' asked Mike curtly.

'Yes,' said Gaby, pushing a button.

'Then let's go,' said Mike with enthusiasm.

Gaby had already been setting the course so merely had to push the boost button – and off they shot at an incredible three and a half miles an hour – interstellar hours, that is.

From the entrance of the cave in which they are sheltering the Adam family, tired and miserable, watch the world's first UFO disappear into space.

CHAPTER II

Godawful

ive minutes later (space-time) the ship was back again.

'Down to Earth,' said Mike, his voice box distorting badly.

'You male-gender models are all the same,' chided Gaby. 'Five minutes on Venus and you go all to pieces – here!' and she spun him round, opened his vox box and made a minor adjustment with the platinum screwdriver at the end of a fingernail. 'There,' she said to an unusually silent Mike. 'Say aaah!'

'Aaah,' said Mike obediently.

'That's better,' said Gaby, slamming his back panel shut a mite harder than necessary.

'I think,' said Mike falteringly, 'I think it's something in her atmosphere that . . . '

'Turns you on.'

'Yeah, just like Pluto turns you on,' retaliated Mike.

'Can you connect me to the Eden satellite?' cut in Gaby curtly.

'Haven't you forgotten one little word?' taunted Mike.

'Can you connect me to the Eden satellite, *please*,' growled Gaby.

'That's better,' said Mike with a mechanical smile. Then *click* as the satellite beamed in a picture of Eden, which was now a desert.

'No sign of them,' said Mike.

'Small wonder,' replied Gaby. 'They were never programmed to digest sand. Hey, what's that? Zoom in!' Mike does so, revealing a camel train.

'So at least they've discovered a primitive mode of transport,' observed Mike.

'No sign of the wheel yet though,' said Gaby sadly, 'but what's the writing on that rock?' Mike zoomed in even tighter to reveal the engraving on a wayside rock. 'Jerusalem fifty-three miles. What's a miles?' she queried.

'Miles is an old Anglo-Saxon name,' said Mike, 'but what fifty-three of them are doing over here so far from home only Rossum knows. But what's a Jerusalem?'

Gaby activated her Q & A cells and immediately came up with the answer. 'Jerusalem, Jerusalem artichoke – vegetable commonly grown in the environs of Jerusalem . . . '

Mike reacted excitedly. 'Query Jerusalem.'

Another check and Gaby spouted the answer. 'Holy City fifty-three miles east of Eden.'

'Now find out . . . ?'

Way ahead of him, Gaby snapped, 'Miles, Anglo-Saxon name also plural of mile – one thousand seven hundred and sixty consecutive paces of the average human male animal.'

'Seems an arbitrary sort of measurement,' said Mike.

'It's obviously a male-dominated society down there,' said Gaby. 'My reasoning would be that a woman really invented the mile and came up with two thousand female paces, a good round figure, but as usual man stuck his foot in and took all the credit.'

Mike's metal lips tightened a millimetre but, as he had his back to Gaby while he was setting a course for Jerusalem, what she didn't know couldn't hurt her.

'There's a wheel,' exclaimed Gaby excitedly, looking through the porthole of the spaceship as it zoomed over Jerusalem, billiseconds later.

' . . . And another, and another,' echoed Mike, excited as a schoolboy.

'Hey, seems we're in there with a chance, maybe one day *they will* invent an antidote to the deadly virus threatening the entire Robot Race.'

'It's up to us to see they do,' said Mike, going into 'real earnest' mode.

And they both fell silent, their individual thought patterns causing their big round eyes to glow with 'hope' mode.

So what did the video recorders in their metallic craniums register as they beamed down on Jerusalem that sunny day in the spring of zero BC? Well, it was much as you'd expect, if you are at all familiar with the Hollywood Biblical epic – and can there be one solitary soul on the entire planet who has not seen either Cecil B. de Mille's *Ten Commandments*, *Ben Hur* (loved him, hated her), *The Bible*, *The Robe*, *Demetrius and the Gladiator*, *Quo Vadis* or even *The Life of Brian*, come to that.

Yes, it seemed like a UFO's view of any Hollywood film set teeming with extras dressed in sheets and sandals with tea towels on their heads and a few Roman soldiers thrown in for good measure, all jostling and gesticulating for all they are worth, just a second after the director calls 'action'.

But what did the denizens of Jerusalem see if they happened to glance skyward in the direction of those mechanical observers hovering only a few hundred feet above their heads?

Well, they saw nothing, absolutely nothing at all – for the simple reason that the material from which the A.R.K. 2001 was constructed was not always subject to the laws governing the frequency of light – invisibility was an optional extra. Simple as that!

'Well, this is all very picturesque but I guess it's time we did our homework,' said Mike. 'Time to play back the real-time recorder.'

'B-O-R-I-N-G,' said Gaby, simulating a yawn.

'Don't worry,' replied Mike, 'we can always "fast-forward".'

'Are your memory cells playing up again?' said Gaby.

'I'm not programmed to worry. You're the worrier, remember.'

'As if I could ever forget,' moaned Mike, programming the playback.

And as the tape started to roll, unfolding the history of the human race before their very eyes, Mike's 'worry capacity unit' began peaking dangerously close to overload while Gaby's 'expectation scanner' plummeted ominously close to zero. For what they saw in the five space-seconds it took them to get the picture spelt the premature end of the human race and consequently their own. From the very moment Cain killed Abel it was clear the species was doomed.

'There's a fundamental design fault there somewhere,' said Mike, as the time recorder reached 'now' and automatically switched off. Then silence as Gaby's sophisticated computer system rapidly considered the options – all of which came up with the same solution.

'I guess there's only one word for it,' said Gaby, looking sadly at Mike, who gazed back even more sadly.

'*Abort*,' they uttered simultaneously.

Another pause and Gaby said, 'Who's going to break the news to Rossum?'

"He'll go apeshit,' prophesied Mike. 'He spent years perfecting those humans. The culmination of a lifetime's dedicated work.'

'So what'll happen to us?' asked Gaby.

'The same thing that happens to any piece of equipment that fails to meet its specifications,' said Mike. 'Obsolescence.'

'The scrap heap.' And once again they spoke with one voice.

'So who's going to break the news to the boss?' asked Gaby.

'Perhaps we're throwing in the towel too early,' said Mike, who Rossum had programmed with a degree more circumspection than Gaby.

'So what do you propose?' retorted Gaby, who was programmed with several more degrees of practicality.

'Well, we could maybe try and find the cause of the malfunction and, er . . . fix it,' said Mike tentatively.

'Just like that,' said Gaby, snapping her elegant fingers.

'Well, we know the root cause of it is down to negative interference by the alien,' said Mike.

'Which Rossum had no way of predicting,' said Gaby. 'I guess we should have zapped that little insect at the very start.'

'And run the risk of an intergalactic war,' said Mike, shaking his shiny old head.

'So what's his little game?' asked Gaby.

'Who knows,' replied Mike. 'Maybe he was just taking advantage of our experiment to test a theory of his own.'

'And blow ours in the process.'

'Maybe it's not beyond salvation,' said Mike hopefully.

'I'd say it was a complete destruction and redesign job,' replied Gaby.

'Not necessarily,' said Mike. 'Humans are highly intelligent creatures capable of an almost infinite range of ideas and emotions to which the alien added a couple more – as yet unclassified.'

'Don't tell me, let me guess,' urged Gaby, switching rapidly to 'random mode'. 'They must be, er . . . give me a clue, quick.'

'We don't have words to express them,' said Mike with the merest hint of a smile.

'That's obvious,' said Gaby with a grin. 'Then those far-out human feelings you're referring to must be what *they* call sin and guilt.'

'Got it,' beamed Mike.

'But they're handling those already,' Gaby pointed out. 'They've dreamed up all those funny old Gods expressly to forgive them their sins and remove the guilt.'

'Well, they can just dream on,' said Mike, 'coz they've got a long wait.'

'Give them a break,' said Gaby, 'they're still at a primitive stage of development. As they come to understand the nature of the universe they'll stop relying on spooky magic and come to believe in the ultimate truth – science.'

'A-Rossum,' said Mike, reverently bowing his head.

'But how are they going to live in harmony with the universe if they can't even live in harmony with each other?' wondered Gaby aloud.

'Though it's clearly what they want,' said Mike, 'or they wouldn't always be praying to their so-called Gods.'

'And what Gods!' said Gaby vehemently. 'Cats, dogs, clouds, bushes, birds and Rossum knows what. And what do they imagine all these Gods demand for their divine intervention?'

'Tell me,' said Mike.

'Blood,' Gaby replied. 'Burnt offerings, blood sacrifices – kids of both varieties, lambs, sheep, rams and even sacred cows.'

'Not sacred cows surely, sweetie,' said Mike, slipping in a rare term of endearment in order to soften the note of criticism in his voice.

My Rossum! Was Gaby's face red. This was the very first time in all the aeons they'd been a team that Mike had voiced anything in the least way personal.

'Er, where were we?' said Mike in the ensuing silence. But Gaby did not respond – her circuits had all overheated and tripped out until such time as she cooled down again. And that moment's silence gave Mike a chance to think. Then it came to him in a flash and *his* circuits blew – with embarrassment. Such energy surges were rare in a model of Mike's mental capacity and soon *he* was switched off and simmering down. In the event, Gaby was the first one to reactivate and completely misconstrued Mike's static state.

'Sweetie,' she murmured, 'sweetie, he called me sweetie for the first time in aeons – no wonder our circuits blew. I always did think he was cute, but he's cuter than ever with his mouth closed.'

Mike's mouth clicked open a moment later and the spell was broken. 'Where were we?' he asked. 'Oh yes, animal sacrifices.'

'They're obviously not into animal rights yet,' Gaby replied, playing along.

'Do y'know what I think?' said Mike, switching to 'revolutionary mode'.

'Tell me,' said Gaby, glowing expectantly.

'I think that neither of us is ready for the scrap heap,' said Mike resolutely. 'I think we should fight this thing. There's gotta be a way we can get these guys back on course, get them back in touch with their true natures again and harness all that mental energy to positivity and progress before they blow themselves to bits.'

'And us with them,' added Gaby. 'So what's the solution?'

'The solution,' said Mike in a manner that could only be described as 'breathless', 'is to give them a God of our own devising. A God that will save them instead of scaring them. You've seen how they grovel before their Gods, whatever their shape or size.'

'Yeah, they're all scared shitless,' said Gaby, betraying once again the social origins of her programmer.

'Exactly,' said Mike, invisibly wincing. 'They go in fear and trembling of their Gods of Wrath. We will give them a God of Love.'

'Crazy man,' said Gaby. 'And just how do you propose we do that?'

'Look,' said Mike, carried away by his own enthusiasm. 'Which of all their Gods do you find the most plausible?'

'The God of the Jews,' said Gaby without hesitation.

'Why?' asked Mike.

'Why? I'll tell you why,' said Gaby. 'Because he's got a sense of humour, that's why – getting them out of a hole one minute and kicking the shit out of them the next.'

'And what about the Ten Commandments?' said Mike.

'You mean the laws Moses dreamed up on Mount Sinai? We only have his word that he heard the voice of God, no one else in the tribe heard it.'

'They were too busy making whoopee down below,' said Mike.

'And what was the first thing Moses did when he got off the mountain? He broke law number six.'

'Thou shall not kill,' said Mike solemnly.

'Wiped out all the ravers, every last one. Pure envy,' said Gaby.

'Thus breaking the last Commandment at the same time,' added Mike.

'The man was a schizophrenic,' said Gaby forcibly. 'Hearing voices and talking to someone who ain't there are two sure signs.'

'All the same, the Commandments themselves weren't half bad,' offered Mike tentatively.

'If anybody could ever live up to them,' said Gaby.

'They need someone to set them a fresh example,' said Mike, 'someone to inspire them, someone they can believe in.'

'Well, Moses had his shot and he blew it,' said Gaby. 'No one's going to believe in any fuddy duddy old judge with a long grey beard any more; the kids of today only look to their own generation. They follow their own star.'

'And we're gonna make that star, make it happen,' enthused Mike.

'How?' said Gaby.

'Don't the Jews believe their God is going to come down one day and walk among them like a man?'

'According to Isaiah they do,' said Gaby, pausing for a
split second to run through the Book of that Prophet
and quoting 'Prepare the way of the Lord'.

'Coz here he comes,' continued Mike, his glass eyes
glowing.

'And when he does he'll need a sidekick, a mouthpiece "crying out in the wilderness" – that's also part of
the prophecy,' said Gaby.

'Great, we'll fix that too,' said Mike, 'then they'll really
believe Isaiah's prophecy has come to pass.'

'So what's the scam?' asked Gaby. 'Do we send back to
base for a couple of fully-grown models and zap 'em
with pre-programmed microchips? We could have 'em
preaching our doctrine within a week!'

Mike's face registered doubt. 'A couple of strangers
suddenly happening on the scene straight out of the
blue . . . ? Mm, I don't think they'd buy it.'

'You think they'd suspect a set-up?' said Gaby.

'Wouldn't you?' asked Mike.

'I think the whole damn thing's crazy,' said Gaby,
beginning to lose patience.

'I know it's a long shot but bear with me a minute and
I'll explain.'

'I'm listening,' said Gaby, registering scepticism.

'This guy has to be someone special,' said Mike,
'someone with class, real class, someone with a
respected family tree and Kosher parents.'

'I've got the very man for the father,' said Gaby, after
only the briefest pause. 'Joseph Heli, whose old man was
known as Matthat, son of Levi, son of Melchi, son of
Jannai, son of Joseph, son of Matthathias, son of Amos,

son of Nathum, son of Esli, son of Naggat, son of Maath, son of Mattathias, son of Semein, son of Josein, son of Joda, son of Joanan, son of Rhesa, son of Zerubbabel, son of Shealtiel, son of Neti, son of Melchi, son of Addi, son of Cosam, son of Elinadam, son of Er, son of Joshua, son of Eliezer, son of Jorim, son of Matthat, son of Levi, son of Simeon, son of Judah, son of Joseph, son of Jonam, son of Eliakim, son of Melea, son of Menna, son of Mattatha, son of Nathan, son of David, son of Jesse, son of Obed, son of Boaz, son of Sala, son of Nahshon, son of Amminadab, son of Admin, son of Arni, son of Hezron, son of Perez, son of Judah, son of Jacob, son of Isaac, son of Abraham, son of Terah, son of Nahor, son of Serug, son of Ren, son of Peleg, son of Eber, son of Shelah, son of Cainan, son of Arphaxad, son of Shem, son of Noah, son of Lamech, son of Methuselah, son of Enoch, son of Jared, son of Mahalaleel, son of Cainan Enos, son of Seth, son of Adam. Howzat!'

'Who's Joseph Heli?' asked Mike.

'Who's Joseph Heli? Is that all you can say?' piped Gaby, her piquemeter peaking out. 'Who's Joseph Heli?'

'I meant to s – say "impressive",' stammered Mike, 'but I guess my data-storage unit was still running. Anyway, what I meant to say was what does he do for a living?'

'I think you're in need of a good overhaul,' said Gaby heatedly, automatically tripping-in her supercooling system. 'Joseph Heli's a carpenter in a small line of business in Nazareth,' she continued more calmly, adding, 'Well, I'm glad you found my read-out impressive.'

'I sure did,' replied Mike eagerly. 'Let's go for it. We've selected the Messiah's father, now what about his mother?'

'We need to find us a nice Jewish princess,' said Gaby, folding her arms with authority.

To Mike she looked the very image of a Yiddisha Momma but he wisely refrained from saying so.

CHAPTER III

Holy Intercourse

s things turned out, Joseph Heli already had a girlfriend. True, she wasn't a princess but she was a good Jewish girl from a respectable family. Her name was Mary. Gaby was disappointed.

'But she's a shepherdess and such a plain name – Mary.'

'What's wrong with Mary?' questioned Mike.

'Mary had a little lamb . . . the doctor fainted,' quipped Gaby. 'Now, with a princess for a mother our Messiah would command some respect.'

'But where are we going to find a Jewish princess willing to marry a poor carpenter?' asked Mike. 'And

more to the point where in all Israel are we going to
find a Jewish princess who is still a virgin? That's part of
the prophecy too, remember?'

Gaby was stymied, Mike was right. How to save face?
Her rationalising circuits worked overtime. 'There's also
the Messiah's mouthpiece to consider,' she said, evading direct confrontation. 'He's got to be pretty special
too.'

'So?' said Mike, just a millivolt impatiently.

'So,' replied Gaby, just two millivolts snappily, 'in
checking out Mary's personal data-bank it seems she's
related to a very holy man – her Uncle Zachariah is a
priest in the Temple.'

'So?' said Mike again, his cooling system going flat
out.

'So he would make a wonderful father for the
Messiah's mouthpiece.'

'But what's that got to do with Mary?' said Mike, in
danger of tripping into exasperation mode.

'Well, it's nice to keep it all in the family,' said Gaby by
way of explanation.

Realising he was in a no-win situation Mike let it
pass. Meanwhile the subjects of their concern went
about their business as usual. Joseph put the finishing
touches to a cross in his carpenter's shop. Mary started
to bring her father's sheep down from the hills above
Nazareth and old Zachariah the priest checked in for a
spell of night duty at the local Temple. It was there
Mike and Gaby picked him up on the odourometer.
This was a means of identification even more accurate than fingerprinting and a darn sight quicker than

DNA testing. For as every dog knows (and every R.U.R. Mark II, come to that) every creature on Rossum's Earth had its own individual scent and, having got a fix on his home and sampled Zachariah's nightshirt, they were able to pinpoint his whereabouts in milliseconds.

'A little older than I expected,' said Gaby tentatively as they observed Zachariah tottering into the sanctuary.

'Older! This guy makes Methuselah look like a toy boy,' exclaimed Mike in a rare burst of exaggeration. He should have put his foot down earlier. This was the last time he'd give in to Gaby just to keep the peace. Gaby was contrite.

'Maybe we should blow him out,' she offered.

'If we're going to give up this easily we're going to get nowhere fast,' said Mike flatly.

'Sorry,' said Gaby. Mike jumped physically. In all the light years he'd known Gaby he had never heard her say that word. Heck! He didn't even know she was programmed to say that word. Nor was he programmed to respond to it – so he said nothing. Neither did he make a remark as old Zach fumbled with his matches in trying to ignite the incense. Nor did Gaby, they were both under a lot of pressure. But when old Zach finally managed to light the match and the whole box spilt on the floor they both hooted simultaneously as their pressure gauges literally let off steam – yes, steam.

Not so very strange when one remembers, as was mentioned earlier, that the cabin owed more to Captain Nemo than Yuri Gagarin. And by the time old Zach had got it together, lit the incense and literally dropped to his knees to pray our Robots were ready for him. First Gaby nodded to Mike who activated the angel hologram in the clouds of rising incense, and then Mike nodded to Gaby who cleared her throat and spoke into the microphone beamed to the mouth of the angel.

And what did the angel look like? You may well ask. Realising that every individual had a different picture of an angel in their mind's eye, the Robots had decided to run a quick brain scan of the subject in question and project the appropriate image with just enough enhancement to impress the subject without giving him a heart attack. And Zach's idea of an angel was Moses with wings so that is what he saw, although he had never imagined the prophet naked with a large erect penis.

Zach fainted.

'Shit, we blew it,' exclaimed Gaby. 'Do you think the wings are too much? I forgot they have no knowledge of dinosaurs.'

'Maybe we should swap the pterodactyl's wings for something more bird-like,' suggested Mike. 'And while we're at it, let's do something about that penis.'

'That was meant to give him ideas,' said Gaby, getting to work on her computer graphics.

'Yeah, the wrong sort of ideas,' said Mike. 'The last thing we want is a gay priest on our hands. So kill that hard-on and get him into something more respectable.'

And by the time old Zach came to, Gaby had done just that. And this time he remained conscious as he took in the vision – of the benign figure of a bearded old man in a white robe hovering on a cloud of incense, fluffy wings a-fluttering. The vision spoke in a sweet soprano.

'I am the Archangel Gabriella,' she said. 'And have I got news for you!'

Back in the spaceship Mike gave Gaby a nudge. 'Drop your vox box a couple of octaves and cut the vernacular.'

Gaby nodded, made the necessary adjustments to the vox box, turned her talk mode to Biblespeak and continued in deeper and more measured tones. 'Your wife shall bear you a son and you shall name him John. Through him you will know great joy and happiness and he shall bring the word of God to the hearts of the people. Now get thee hence to thy dwelling place and fucketh your old woman,' said Gaby with a frown as the tuner began to drift towards the vernacular again.

'But my wife is barren and I and I . . . I . . . '

'Oh, for God's sake spit it out, man,' shouted Gaby. 'Doest thou mean, old fart, that thou cannest not get it up?'

Whereupon old Zach was struck dumb with shame.

'Shit, I screwed up again,' said Gaby, turning to Mike but forgetting to kill the transmitter. And as Zach fled in terror, Mike deactivated the transmitter and brought his 'fixed smile' circuit into action.

'That's perfectly OK, sweetie,' he crooned. 'Just stick to the script a bit more and go easy on the ad libs, that's all. A few more rehearsals and you'll be absolutely fine.'

A fresh endearment and no reproaches – this was a new Mike speaking and one she could learn to go for. She didn't know just how close to the mark she was. Mike, realising that the strain of what they were going through was over and above their normal workload potential, was reprogramming his entire R.U.R. response system with what appeared to be quite promising results. But there was a limit to what was permissible, for initiative had been known to lead to anarchy and its inevitable consequence – termination. Perhaps deep down in her complex brain Gaby sensed this and her response patterns were being subconsciously reprogrammed accordingly. Unbeknown to them this was something of a technological breakthrough.

And as it turned out getting old Zach's barren old wife, Elizabeth, pregnant was not nearly as problematic as they feared. Teleporting and implanting a basic fertility drug did wonders for her ovaries, and jazzing up Zach's sex drive by sending him a nocturnal vision of the hottest belly dancer in Istanbul and zapping his night-time cup of cocoa with a dash of Spanish fly was a pushover, resulting in the best sex they'd had in over eighty years.

So much for the first part of the prophecy – now for the second. And although it was really Mike's turn to play the angel, Gaby cajoled him into giving her another chance. Mike saw it as a means of restoring her self-esteem and gave her the go-ahead, for which Gaby was grateful.

*

The odourometer located Joe and Mary on a hillside above Nazareth, surrounded by sheep – a couple of happy teenagers very much in love. He, the typical football hero, she, the cutest girl on the block. And, to continue our movie analogy, if you starred the young Dustin Hoffman as Joe and the young Jennifer Jones as Mary you'd have the makings of a big box-office blockbuster. And that's who they looked like.

'What d'ya say to coming over to my place tonight, honey?' said Joe with a sexy smile.

'Tonight I have to babysit. Pappa's taking Momma to the theatre,' said Mary. 'Besides, you know they don't like me out nights.'

'It's just I got somethin' to show you, somethin' I've been workin' on nights for the past couple months,' said Joe. 'It's sort of a surprise.'

'So that's why you haven't been hanging around lately,' said Mary coyly. 'Momma was beginning to think you were giving me the go by.'

'What did *you* think?' asked Joe, brushing her cheek with a blade of grass.

'Tell me,' said Mary, evading the question, 'what's this surprise?'

'Come see for yourself,' Joe teased.

'Give me a clue,' Mary replied.

'It's a wedding present.'

'Is this your subtle way of proposing?' She laughed.

'If you guess right you'll know soon enough,' he said with a chuckle.

'Well, since you're a carpenter I guess it's something for the home.'

'Warm,' he said.

'If you'd had your way it could have been a cradle. But since you never got to first base—' Suddenly she gets it. 'Oh, Joe, it's not a bed?' she said, laughing and blushing at the same time.

'It's a bed in a million,' exclaimed Joe, 'made of cedar of Lebanon and inlaid with rosewood and mother of pearl. And it's king-sized. And I've even made a first down payment on a camel-hair mattress.'

'And now shall I tell you something?' said Mary, fair bubbling over.

'Why, yeah, sure,' said Joe, a little taken aback.

'I've been making a quilt. It's sky blue with the sun and the moon in pure silk. Of course, it's only queen-sized but I can soon fix that with a border of stars. Oh, Joe, I'm so happy.' Tears of joy fill her eyes, and not for the first time Joe is overwhelmed by her youthful passion and enthusiasm. A moment later they are in each other's arms, hugging, kissing, loving.

'Time we went into action,' said Mike up in A.R.K. 2001, 'or we might have to find ourselves a fresh virgin.'

'No problem,' said Gaby, the corners of her mouth turning up in a cute little mechanical smile, which, rather to his surprise, Mike found not a little sexy as he watched her get to work on programming a pretty hologram angel with nice feathery wings which were destined to become a prototype for generations of angels to come. Snapping out of it, Mike aimed his solar stun-gun at one of the grazing sheep and set it to transmit a mild electric shock. *Zap! Baa!* Mild, but sufficiently strong to send it scampering up the hill with Mary in close pursuit . . . leaving poor Joe all hot and bothered.

'Wait for me,' he shouted as an afterthought.

'No, you stay put and keep an eye on the others. I'll soon take care of this little guy,' she shouted back, following it around a pile of boulders just in time to see it trot through a fissure in the rocks. She hurried after it, squeezing her way through. *Pow!* A blinding light hit her as she stepped into a natural amphitheatre of stone the colour of ivory. But if the sheep was there she didn't see it, hypnotised as she was by the pulsating light which was gradually forming into . . . what . . . ? Was it a bird, was it a man . . . ?

'Hi, Mary, stay cool. I'm your Guardian Angel. My name is Gabriel and I bring you greetings from God who has chosen you above all other women to be the mother of his beloved Son.'

Mary was so stunned by the beauty of this angel, with the most kindly smile she had ever seen, that she could barely take in what he was saying.

'And you shall be possessed by the Holy Spirit and give birth to a boy.'

'Are you telling me I've been dating God when all the time I thought it was Joe?' queried Mary. 'Is *he* the Holy Spirit?'

'Certainly not,' said the voice of Gaby, losing her angelic tone for a moment.

'Then how is this possible?'

'Don't ask,' said Gaby a mite feistily. 'With God, all things are possible.'

At this, Gaby pushed the pause button (which put Mary's consciousness on hold) and turned to Mike.

'She's not responding quite as we figured,' said Gaby. 'She's putting us on the spot.'

'Give me a second and I'll have teleported the DNA Supersperm to her womb . . . Five, four, three, two, one. Blast off.'

'Yes,' shouted Gaby as a loud clang registered a direct hit.

A beat later, Gaby released the pause button and Mike deactivated the hologram and reactivated Mary.

Fzzzz/phtt, wow, wow, wow, meaoww, splutter, splutter . . . then silence as the video screen faded to black. And that was the last Mike and Gaby were to see of their protégée for nigh on nine months.

They looked at each other open-mouthed, and if it had been possible for them to do so they would have turned a lighter shade of pale.

'The entire video system has gone down,' said Mike.

'Including the back-up system,' said Gaby.

'And even the back-up system to the back-up system,' added Mike. 'We'll need a complete refit.'

'So it's back to base,' said Gaby, setting a course for home.

'Well, at least we tied up phase one,' said Mike.

'Pity we can't stay around for the fireworks,' said Gaby.

'Fireworks?' queried Mike.

'When she tells him she's pregnant,' said Gaby.

Whoosh – up and away.

*

'Look, a shooting star,' said Mary, pointing to the sky as she returned to Joseph with the reclaimed sheep.

'What on earth have you been up to?' asked Joe, ignoring her observation.

'Having intercourse with God,' she said, with a broad smile that seemed to take in the entire universe.

CHAPTER IV

Virgin Birth
at the
Holy Day Inn

By the time our metallic duo picked them up again on the road to Bethlehem Mary was about to give birth. She looked tired and so did the donkey on which she was riding and so did Joe, who was leading it, laden down with provisions.

'Well, they're still together,' said Mike with some relief as he tuned into their wavelength and they came into focus on a state-of-the-art spherical 3-D monitor screen in radioactive Rossumcolour.

'But what are they doing on the road to Bethlehem?' asked Gaby. 'She should be in bed back home in Nazareth.'

Knowing they would find out sooner or later, Mike left the question unanswered.

Down below, a cloud of dust in the distance was rapidly gaining on the young couple. As it got closer it became recognisable as an opulent carriage drawn by four sweating horses.

'Out of the way, beggars!' yelled the driver. 'Make way for the high priest Caiaphas.'

The donkey gave a squeal of fright and tried to scramble up the steep bank, pitching Mary on to the stones. The wheels flashed by only inches from her head. And as Mary coughed and spluttered in the dust, Caiaphas looked out of the rear window of the receding carriage and laughed fit to bust. Joseph, consumed with road rage, hurled a brick at him but it fell well short of the mark and only succeeded in getting another disparaging laugh from the culprit.

'Fine way to treat the mother of God,' Joe muttered, turning to help Mary to her feet, but whether he was being facetious or caring it was difficult to say. 'Are you hurt, honey?' he asked with real concern.

To his surprise Mary laughed and said, 'No.'

'What's so funny?' asked Joe.

'He called us beggars, when we have riches beyond his wildest dreams,' replied Mary.

Joseph helped her back on to the donkey and discreetly changed the subject.

'Don't worry, another hour or so and we should be checking into the hotel and then it's a nice hot bath and a good night's sleep for you, m'lady.'

'How long will the census take tomorrow?' asked

Mary, as Joseph shouldered his heavy bag and started to lead the donkey along the winding way.

'Depends on how many officials they've hired to handle the register,' he replied. 'Why?'

'I'd like the child to be born back home in Nazareth,' said Mary.

'Well, don't blame me if he isn't,' said Joe. 'I was born in Bethlehem, I have to be counted in Bethlehem. I'm not doing this for my health, believe me. And the priests say Moses delivered us from slavery. Bullshit, we're still slaves and always will be . . .'

'Oh, Joe, give me a break, will you?' said Mary wearily. 'You were only too glad to get out of Nazareth. You're ashamed of me, admit it. Am I to blame if they don't believe the truth?'

'No!' said Joe with some heat. '*I'm* the one to blame and no one in town will let me forget it. They're convinced the kid is mine and the only reason we got married was to make it legit. Then you go around saying it's not mine and that God is the father. Either way I'm a loser – I either seduced a young chick or I married a crazy one.'

Mary was silent. Joe glanced over his shoulder, saw she was weeping and immediately became remorseful.

'Sorry, honey,' he muttered, 'don't worry . . . I believe you.'

'That's all right, Joe,' said Mary, 'you'll see . . . ' And they continued the journey in silence. In the sky the first evening star appeared. To Mary it almost seemed to be following them, though she wisely refrained from mentioning it to Joe.

*

And up in the spaceship that Mary took for a star the Robots read her thoughts and reacted fast.

'Quick, hit the light-deflector switch,' shouted Mike.

'Sorry, it was still set up for deep space,' said Gaby, hitting the switch that would render the ship invisible to the naked eye once more.

Mary was glad she hadn't mentioned it to Joe.

'Spunky girl,' remarked Gaby.

'Adorable,' said Mike, causing Gaby to raise one of the fine metal brushes that constituted her eyebrows.

'What do you mean "adorable"? You'll be "worshipping" her next. Your word bank is in need of dehumanising.'

Mike said nothing; for once he was at a loss for words. In contrite mode, Gaby helped him out. 'Time for a little shuteye. Shall I take the first watch . . . honey?' she said, slipping into earthling lovespeak to make him feel better.

It worked. Mike nodded, switched on a smile and shut down.

'Men!' thought Gaby to herself as she went about her business of monitoring the holy couple. And as she fine-tuned the odourometer it picked them up loud and clear at the reception area of the Holy Day Inn, Bethlehem – which might best be described as a suburb of Jerusalem.

'I'm sorry, we've had to let your room go, sir,' said a rather harassed-looking man behind the desk. 'Reservations are cancelled automatically if guests fail to check in by six p.m.'

'But we had a breakdown, my donkey went lame or somethin' and my wife had to walk. She's expecting a baby.'

'I'm sorry, sir, I really am. It's the census, there's not a single bed to be had in all of Bethlehem. People are being turned away in droves.'

'Let me see the manager,' shouted Joe in frustration.

'You're looking at him, sir,' came the icy reply, 'and unless you leave quietly I shall have you escorted from the premises.'

'What's the problem, Joe?' said Mary.

'Full house, we've been gazumped,' Joe replied. 'This creep is throwing us out.' Then to the manager, 'Do you realise what you are doing? You are turning the mother of God out into the streets.'

The manager was freaked. People gathering in the foyer were freaked. The burly porter was freaked too but got ready to evict the crazy guy – just awaiting a nod from the boss. Then Mary spoke again.

'It's the donkey, she's in a bad way, I doubt if she'll last the night. Is there a vet you could recommend and perhaps a local stable? It's just started to rain.'

Everyone, including Joseph, was gobsmacked. The manager was particularly moved. He'd had difficult customers before, had them most every day in fact . . . but the pregnant woman putting a crummy donkey before her own comfort was something completely new to him.

'There's a manger in back of the hotel by the parking

lot,' the manager found himself saying. 'You can have the use of that.'

'And don't forget,' interjected the porter, 'it's for the use of animals only.'

But the manager overrode him. 'They've got to nurse the sick animal, don't they, leastwise till the vet comes. Now show them the way; then fix them up with something to eat. Then go get the vet, pronto.'

Mary said nothing but gave the manager a smile. A smile he would never forget.

'How much?' said Joseph.

'It's on the house,' said the manager. 'And I apologise for the inconvenience.'

Then, almost brusquely, as if half regretting his generosity, he turned abruptly to the next customer as the porter, puzzled by the manager's action, led the happy couple away, watched by the curious bystanders.

Ten thousand feet above them things are buzzing as Mike, switched on again, gives voice to his thoughts. 'And we shall shine like the brightest star in the firmament as a sign to all mankind that the time of their deliverance is at hand.'

Gaby stares at him, open-mouthed.

'Just rehearsing,' says Mike. 'Now it's my turn to play. Prepare for maximum solarisation.'

With a sigh of relief Gaby busies herself at the control panel. 'For a moment you had me worried, I thought I was listening to the God of Moses there.'

'That's the idea,' says Mike. 'Glory to the Lord on High and on Earth peace and goodwill to all,' he declaims.

A cry of joy suffused with pain draws them to the monitor where on a bed of straw in the manger, surrounded by the animals, Mary is about to give birth. Joseph holds his breath while the vet yells, 'Bear down, nearly there . . . push . . . push!'

'Hallelujah,' shouts Mike as the Messiah's head appears between Mary's legs, causing Gaby to look at him in wonder. But that's not all. When the Messiah gives his first cry, after the vet has held him up by the ankles and given him a slap, everything on the monitor screen gradually becomes infused with a golden glow which even appears in the ship itself as every monitor on board radiates an intense golden light.

R.U.R.s are programmed not to panic, so Mike and Gaby take this unprecedented phenomenon as a mechanical rather than a supernatural one and set about investigating the cause.

' . . . Better put us on course for the manger,' says Mike after a while.

'Whatever for?' asks Gaby.

'We've got to let everyone know he's arrived,' says Mike.

'Are you out of your mind?' says Gaby. 'He'll be killed in the rush.'

Mike's response system automatically switches off. It is the human equivalent of being stunned. Her remarks are over-emotional and insubordinate. Worse still they make sense. His word processor filters his response carefully.

'Correction, reset course for destination five miles due west of city centre, altitude five hundred feet.'

Gaby turns a dial and they are there less than a moment later.

'Check,' she says flatly, regretting her insubordination.

'Are those human shapes on the hillside directly below us?' asks Mike.

'Confirm,' says Gaby after an uncharacteristically long delay.

'Are you having a problem?' asks Mike.

'It's the odourometer,' replies Gaby. 'There's so much sheep shit around the stench is killing everything else. I'd say there were four or five humans down there, shepherds most likely.'

'Stand by for voice transmission,' says Mike.

'No angel hologram?' queries Gaby.

'No, tonight I'm going for a talking star,' says Mike.

'They'll never believe it,' says Gaby.

'Let's give it a whirl anyway,' says Mike authoritatively. 'What have we got to lose?'

Gaby could give him numerous suggestions but wisely remains silent and obeys orders.

Five hundred feet below the five shepherds gazed up at the pulsating star whose erratic course they had been following with growing wonder. It was truly awesome. And when a deep, resonant voice emanated from its shining light – positively astounding.

'Be not afraid,' boomed Mike's reprocessed voice. 'I bring great news to you personally and to the world in general. A saviour who is Christ the Lord has just been born in Bethlehem in a manger.'

'Manger, schmanger, what manger? There are as

many mangers in Bethlehem as I've had hot gafilterfish,' one of the more practical of the shepherds muttered to himself.

'The manger in the parking lot of the Holy Day Inn,' boomed a slightly exasperated voice from the shining star, before continuing in more even tones, 'He will bring great joy to everyone and his kingdom shall last forever and all nations shall pay homage to him alone and forever bless his name, Christ Jesus, son of the living God – over and out.'

'Over and out, over and out, what is the meaning of this over and out,' the shepherds muttered among themselves as the star faded into darkness and disappeared.

But the message was clear enough and they started drawing lots at once to see who should stay and who should go, but the enigma 'over and out' was to bug them for the rest of their days.

Up inside the darkened spaceship Mike glowed with pride. 'What d'you think?' he asked, turning to Gaby.

'You got real star quality,' she said without a hint of irony, 'but next time you finish the message give me a nod. I'm afraid we transmitted "over and out".'

Slightly miffed, Mike nodded but this hint of criticism wasn't enough to dampen his enthusiasm. 'And in an hour or so they'll see for themselves and so the word will begin to spread.'

'There's just one thing that bothers me,' said Gaby thoughtfully. 'What if the King also got the message? Don't you think he'd be pissed off?'

'Why?' asked Mike.

'Because you just said everyone, *but everyone*, should pay homage to Jesus, including bad King Herod who, judging from his record, is not the type to bend the knee to anyone, let alone some newborn brat in a cow-shed in Bethlehem.' Mike joined her at the character evaluator and what he saw made his circuits race.

'Maybe we should have beamed an audio phase cancellation at Herod's palace,' said Gaby, beginning to regain some of her lost authority.

'Better give me a visual on it – quick,' snapped Mike.

'Speed of light fast enough for you?' retorted Gaby, touching a sensor.

Mike briefly went into glower mode, which cancelled itself out directly Herod's palace flashed up on the big master screen. Simultaneously the golden incandescent glow cut out.

'What did you do?' asked Mike. 'Everything's back to normal.'

'I just changed video channels – maybe it was a loose electron track. I'll check it out.'

CHAPTER V

Star Quality

eanwhile the odourometer had located King Herod in his observatory directly beneath the open dome he used for star-gazing at his palace in Jerusalem. And as the odourzoom moved in closer it revealed the face of a frightened man who might have been a distant ancestor of Woody Allen – even down to the horn-rimmed glasses he used to scan the night sky for signs and omens. Only the clothing and footwear were markedly different, as was to be expected. Dior at Sak's Fifth Avenue – or the Israeli historical equivalent thereof – as opposed to Macy's

bargain basement. And jewellery, the two men were
worlds apart there. I doubt that Woody even sports a
pair of cuff links, whereas Herod's precious stones made
an audible clatter as he shook with fright, mumbling to
himself in the darkness.

'. . . And his Kingdom shall last for ever and all nations
shall pay homage to him alone and . . .'

'Talking to yourself again?' drawls a woman's voice
behind him. His heart sinks. It's his wife – a bit like
Barbra Streisand all dolled up for the Oscars.

'Didn't you hear it? That evil star shining brazenly in
the sky. It's obscured by cloud but listen – it may yet
speak again.'

They listen – nothing. Jezebel decides to humour the
poor man. 'I agree,' she declares impatiently.

'Agree,' says Herod irritably. 'Agree with what?'

'What it says,' snaps Jezebel.

'Says what?' says Herod.

'That you should take me on that Roman holiday you
promised me, and see a good shrink at the same time!'
says Jezebel with a mocking smile.

Tempted to strike her for her impertinence, an act
he would live to regret, Herod subdues his rage as a
shadowy group enters and hovers in the doorway. In
the lead are Herod's two sons. The eldest, Antipas, is a
hunk in his early thirties while his younger brother
Archaelus has all the signs of a downtrodden wimp.
Behind them are three elderly men, humble and travel-
worn. Herod turns towards them with fresh hope. 'Did
you hear it?'

'Hear what, Father?' ventures Archaelus.

'The voice of the star, you fools,' roars Herod.

'The star?' says baffled Archaelus. 'We thought it was you, Father.'

Herod catches Jezebel smirking and is even further enraged. Antipas jumps in to keep the peace.

'We lesser mortals are not blessed with your occult powers, Father, but these learned astrologers have tracked the star all the way from Thebes and think they've got the message.'

'Then let them speak.'

Antipas nods to the eldest of the astrologers who drops to his knees and stammers his message.

'Majesty, it is written in the heavens that a new star of great magnitude shall lead the way to a poor dwelling in a city suburb, where shall be born . . . ' and here he hesitates.

'Go on, go on, man,' shouts Herod impatiently.

But still the astrologer hesitates – until Antipas draws his sword.

' . . . Whence shall be born . . . the King of the Jews,' blurts the astrologer.

Dead silence as Herod visibly pales. This has been the moment Jezebel has been waiting for.

'Darling, why so pale? *You* are the King of the Jews, remember? And all this astrological crap is so old hat, *so* provincial! Nobody in Rome believes in the stars any more, but nobody.'

Herod, lost in a fearsome world of his own, fastens on to the word 'Rome', symbolic of his subjugation to a power greater than his own.

'Rome! This could be Caesar's way of getting rid of

me. Spread rumours of a new King to push me off the throne.'

'And who would he find better suited to rule a land of frightened Jews than the most frightened Jew of them all – tell me?' says Jezebel.

'You'll regret this, woman,' hisses Herod.

'One little shooting star and you're all shitting your-selves,' sneers Jezebel, walking over to the cocktail cabinet to fix herself a drink.

'But, madam,' protests the youngest of the astrologers, 'if you'll forgive me, the stars do not lie, the prophets have always found great wisdom in the stars.'

'Prophets, schmophets,' says Jezebel, knocking back a gin and tonic. 'Uncivilised bunch – they didn't even know the Earth was flat.' And with a toss of her head she exits.

Herod ignores her. Consumed with growing fears he mutters to himself, 'This new star heralds the birth of chaos. I shall be torn apart – Rome pulling me one way and my own people pulling the other – and now the threat to my Kingdom by this brat.' A sinister plan begins to form in his corrupt mind. Hiding his intention he turns to the astrologers, all smiles. 'No, I cannot deny the evidence of my own ears. I believe the prophecy.' And to everyone's surprise he begins collecting a few trinkets scattered about the room which he presses on to the bemused astrologers.

'Here, take these gifts. Go find your King, give him this gold, frankincense and myrrh with my compli-ments. Then come and tell me of his whereabouts that

I may pay homage to him in person.' Sensing danger, the astrologers don't argue and start bowing themselves out.

'It shall be even as you say, O Herod,' says the chief spokesman. When they have gone Antipas summons up the courage to voice his thoughts.

'They won't be back, Father.'

'I know,' says Herod.

'Shall I give orders to have the armed guard follow them, Father?' ventures Archaelus.

'Too clumsy, too noisy,' observes Herod, 'but two serpents gliding through the streets on their bellies . . . ' And he looks at his sons meaningfully . . . until they at last get the message – and don't like it.

'You can't mean us, surely, Father?' says Archaelus with a weak smile.

'You're like your mother, you speak with a forked tongue. And when I'm gone you'll fight over my Kingdom like venomous snakes that strike each other down with poison. Now get moving, for if this brat lives you may have nothing to inherit but ashes.'

And as they go to do his bidding there is silence in the spaceship as the implications hit home.

'It's a bummer,' says Mike finally.

'It stinks,' says Gaby.

'So what's the story, morning glory?' says Mike to Gaby, his 'bold-front' button self-activating. 'Where do we go from here?'

'How about a vacation in Hawaii?' replies Gaby in jokey mode. 'I hear the scuba diving's pretty good.'

'That's OK for you,' replies Mike, eyeing her metallic double-D breast pods, 'you've got built-in buoyancy tanks whereas I've got a big pot to cope with.'

'You could lay on the beach in the sun – bronzing up.'

'If only,' says Mike, 'but, kidding aside, we gotta do something and do it fast.'

'Fine but don't let's lose our cool. Let's get a fix on those scumbags.'

'You mean Herod's kids?' asks Mike.

'Check,' says Gaby.

'Be my guest,' says Mike with unaccustomed chivalry.

Instantaneously the odourometer picks the brothers up lurking behind a chariot in the Holy Day Inn parking lot – just as the three astrologers enter the manger.

'Stay here and keep watch,' says Antipas. 'I'll get back to the palace and alert the old man.'

'But what shall I do if they take a hike?' asks Archaelus anxiously.

'Call a cop and arrest them for vagrancy,' sneers Antipas, taking off into the darkness. Archaelus glowers after him – there is no love lost between them – then turns his attention back to the manger.

In A.R.K. 2001 the interior of the manger flashes on to the master monitor as Gaby anticipates Mike's command. He nods an acknowledgement as they both take in the bizarre sight. It looks like a scene from a Marx Brothers' movie, *A Night at the Opera* to be precise – the scene where a tiny cabin is packed with the Marx Brothers and half the ship's crew, whereas here we have two camels and a mule, Mary winding the baby Jesus, who is screaming his head off, the vet attending the neighing donkey, four shepherds singing 'While Shepherds Watched Their Flocks by Night', and the three astrologers all speaking at once to Joseph who is munching on a camel burger and arguing with the porter. Despite the gravity of the situation Gaby and Mike cannot help but exchange a smile.

Down below Joseph continues haranguing the porter. 'I know very well what I ordered. I ordered one king-size camel burger with extra mayo and a side order of french fries, so help me.'

'What's the matter?' asks the irate porter. 'Are you deaf or just hard of hearing? I told you when you ordered we didn't have any mayo so how can you have *extra* mayo?'

'OK, forget it,' says Joseph, 'I'll settle for ketchup, and make it snappy.'

And as the porter struggles to the door Joseph turns to the astrologers and picks up where they left off.

'But if Herod sends Jesus gifts with one hand why should he threaten his life with the other?'

The chief astrologer tries to convince him. 'Herod is a puppet King despised by his Roman masters and Jewish subjects alike. His balance of power is precarious. He sees in this newborn child a dangerous threat to the throne.'

'Come on, you gotta be kiddin',' exclaims Joseph. 'It's only natural he should wanna pay his respects – but not here, not in a stable.'

Having successfully winded the babe, Mary backs him
up.

'It's we who should go to King Herod. It's clear from
these gifts that he wishes to praise the son of God and
give thanks just like these good shepherds.'

'You're right, of course we should go to the palace,'
says Joe. 'We should have gone there in the first place.
How's the donkey, Doc?'

'Good for another ten thousand miles,' he replies.

'How much do I owe you?' says Joe.

'That'll be twelve shekels for the donkey and for the
birth, well, I usually charge twenty but this is kinda special. I've never handled a virgin birth before so I've no
fixed rate for that, nor actually for bringing a God into
the world neither.'

'This ain't any old God,' protests Joe. 'This here's the
one and only God, the real McCoy.'

'That's a matter of opinion,' says Doc – whereupon
there is a cry of outrage from everyone in the manger,
including the camels. 'All right, all right, so I'm an
agnostic, pardon me for living, so I'm outvoted. So have
this one on me.' Then he turns to the baby as he packs
up his instruments. 'And should you by any chance
really be the living God just remember who brought
you into the world – no forceps and not a mark on you.
And who knows, one day I may need a favour, d'you
hear me?'

'Yeah, I hear you,' says the baby. 'So thank you and
goodnight.' Silence. Everyone is stunned except the
proud parents who can't withhold a giggle.

'Joe's an amateur ventriloquist,' confesses Mary.

'Bar mitzvahs and weddings a speciality. Fifty shekels a show,' says Joe, 'but for you, Doc, it's on the house.' He turns to Mary. 'How you feeling, honey?'

'I'm just fine, Joe, why don't you get along and saddle up?'

Joe blows her a kiss and hurries out.

The wise men are dumbfounded and so are our mechanical friends high above them in the spaceship.

'Well, it's been swell knowing you guys,' says Gaby.

'We gotta to do something to stop that hothead,' says Mike. 'Show him the error of his ways.'

'Shall we take a peep into our crystal ball?' says Gaby.

'It'll use up a helluva lot of energy,' says Mike. 'Maybe we should save it for an emergency.'

All Gaby has to do is raise an elegant eyebrow to convince Mike of the obvious.

'Emergency, emergency, activate Superspace*. Time, maximum fast forward,' he shouts.

'I heard you the first time. No need to dramatise,' says Gaby, her elegant fingers flying over the light-keyboard

---

* *Superspace* – This is eternal and infinite, containing all the universes in existence. Our own time space-time is linked to Superspace by 'worm holes', so although it is apparently a solid fabric (built of geons**) it is in reality a sponge-like structure. It is possible to travel vast distances instantaneously and to travel in time using Superspace.

** *Geons* – Doughnut-shaped masses of mean diameter 10–33 cm. These bundles of energy are the gates to Superspace.

like Elton John playing 'Pinball Wizard'. 'Geonic link stable on monitor two.* Standard time on monitor one,' she exclaims excitedly.

Mike watches her with something akin to confusion. No matter how his currents race he can't analyse his responses. All he knows for sure is that there had been something different about that raised eyebrow. Could it be . . . 'painted'?

Pow! The sudden image of the manger in flames blows it from his mind. He glances at monitor one transmitting standard time where Joe is harnessing the donkey, unaware of what the future holds in store.

'Shall I phase lock?' prompts Gaby.

'Yeah, yeah,' says Mike excitedly.

'Advance time and standard time in lock,' reports Gaby as the lights dim and a curious high-pitched whine becomes audible.

'Oh, my God, Mary,' exclaims Joseph, dropping to his knees in horror.

'What now?' asks Gaby. 'Our energy bank is taking a real hammering.'

'Give me another thirty seconds,' says Mike, 'and hook me up to the molecular terrestaphone.'

'Check,' says Gaby. 'He should hear you loud and clear.'

'Keep cool, Joe, Mary is safe,' declares Mike. 'I am the angel of the Lord and what you see before you is a vision of the future.'

---

* *Monitor two* – The objects appear thinner due to time dilation. (The faster an object travels, the thinner it appears to be.)

'Hurry it up, Mike, for Crissakes,' screams Gaby. 'Another twenty seconds and we're gonna end up a fuckin' satellite circling this dumb planet for ever.'

Mike speeds it up. 'Take your family and flee into Egypt. Herod has murder in his heart.'

'And for Chrissakes hurry,' interjects Gaby, throwing the master-switch with half a second in hand.

And for the next five stellar minutes A.R.K. 2001 was nothing but a ball of scrap metal orbiting the Earth. Even the Robonauts were shut down as the giant solar AAAA batteries slowly recharged themselves. Even the satellite programmed to follow Jesus was affected – which is why so little is known about the Messiah during his formative years.

CHAPTER VI

Hi-Jinks
Over Jordan

rom the Gospels of the Apostles we know that Herod ordered every male child under two years of age living in or around Jerusalem to be butchered. We know that Jesus and his parents escaped into Egypt and that he was a bright but cocky kid.

For example, every year the holy family got together with their friends and neighbours for an outing to Jerusalem to celebrate the Feast of the Passover – and on this particular return journey they suddenly realised Jesus wasn't around. So back to the city they all schlepped and organised a search party. Finally, at their wits' end, Mary decided to try the Temple. And sure enough that's where they found him – discoursing with some priests who were blown away by his wisdom.

'Your mother's been worried sick,' Joseph admonished. 'Is this any way for the son of God to behave? We've been searching high and low for three days now.'

'Gee, I'm sorry, Ma,' said Jesus. 'Sorry, Joe. But didn't you guess I'd be staying at Dad's place?'

Naturally all the priests were righteously miffed. Who did this little smartass think he was, blaspheming in the Temple? And if Joe and Mary hadn't hurried him away God knows what might have happened.

That we know and that's about all. The disciples brush over his teenage years – why? Was he a bit of a tearaway? And as a young man in his twenties, working nine to five in Joe's carpentry shop, what did he do in the evenings – study the scriptures or was he a swinging single into booze and loose women? After all, we are talking about a character manufactured by a couple of Robots from outer space, not some divine spin-off from the Big Bang! Idle speculation. Let's keep to the facts.

The next verifiable fact is that in his thirtieth year Jesus met up with his cousin John on the banks of the River Jordan just where it crosses the main highway from Jericho to Shittim. But our two space angels who engineered the meeting had been planning it ever since the solar batteries had finally recharged and made them fully operational again a couple of years back.

They had brainwashed both men while they slept with a diet of teachings from the Old Testament and nocturnal lectures on man's place in the Universe. All this via microchips implanted in the frontal lobes of their brains.

John the Baptist stood up to his waist in water, facing a thin crowd of bedraggled onlookers on the West Bank. It was pouring with rain, which probably accounted for the poor turnout. But neither factor could diminish the passion of John's commitment as he preached his message while the rain streamed in rivulets down his finely chiselled features – reminiscent of the iron-willed Clint Eastwood in *The Unforgiven*.

Watching him with lustful eyes from the bank, under a golden canopy held by six macho slave boys, is a young thirteen-year-old with all the charm of the teenage Elizabeth Taylor in *National Velvet* and all the sexual charisma of the same star in *Cleopatra*. Her Royal costume isn't that much different either – nor her heavy eye make-up. The name of this Royal sex-slut is Salome. Escorting her entourage of slaves and sycophants is a detachment of Royal guards and a handful of dodgy priests, noting down every word issuing from the prophet's lips.

'Repent, for the Kingdom of Heaven is at hand. So prepare God's Holy Way, make straight the highways, crush the boulders, bridge the valleys, traverse the mountains and you will find the road to eternal salvation.'

A smartly dressed man in a camel-hair overcoat calls to him from the back. 'And what should a rich man do to be saved?'

'Well, for starters,' shouts John, 'you can take that coat off your back and give it to that bag lady beside you.'

'I'll think about it,' drawls the rich man, looking at the bag lady with distaste.

'And how about me?' asks a cynical Roman cavalry officer. 'What should I do to be saved?'

'Rape, pillage and slaughter no more,' commands John, 'for blessed are the peace-makers.'

'And this is the best peace-maker I know,' says the Captain with a smile, drawing his sword.

'Those that live by the sword shall perish by the sword,' says John calmly.

'Remember that if you ever come face to face with a lion in the arena,' snaps the Captain with a grim smile as he sharply reins in his horse and canters away.

The rain stops – encouraging Salome to step out from beneath her canopy. Her entourage go to follow her, but with a brief wave of her hand she halts them and walks down towards the river's edge alone. Then to everyone's surprise she enters the water, fully clothed, wades out to John and looks deeply into his eyes.

'And are you prepared to undertake the long journey to the Kingdom of God, sister?' asks John evenly.

'Why bother when I can find heaven in your arms, lover,' says Salome with a sexy smile. Then to everyone's surprise, John's most of all, she kisses him sensuously on the lips. Quickly recovering, he grabs her roughly by the shoulders and almost spits out his reply.

'The way to salvation lies through the spirit, not by way of the senses!' Then, without warning, he ducks her forcefully under the water saying, 'I baptise you with the Holy Spirit and with fire.' Then he releases her, coughing and spluttering as the heavy mascara runs down her face in black streams. With a cry of rage she stumbles to the bank where she is comforted by her servants. Meanwhile the captain of her bodyguard is confused as to what action to take and does nothing. Not so a group of priests huddled nearby who see this as an opportunity to stir up the gathering crowd against John.

'He's a raving lunatic, a criminal. Don't listen to him. He's just assaulted Princess Salome, daughter of Herod the King,' shouts a furious priest.

John retaliates in a voice of righteous anger. 'Herod Antipas, the adulterer who stole his brother's wife Herodias away from him. Herodias is a whore and the seed of her womb is a slut.'

Salome screams with rage, stirring the captain of the guard into some response. 'Who are you to slander the persons of the Royal household?'

'I am the voice crying in the wilderness as was foretold in the words of Isaiah,' replies John with authority.

It is at this moment he first sees Jesus standing amongst the onlookers gathered on the riverbank. With trembling hand he points him out. 'Behold the son of God who will take away the sins of the world. He is the one I have prophesied: Christ Jesus, our blessed Lord.'

All eyes turn to the charismatic man in a robe of shining white as he strides into the water towards John, looking for all the world like the young Peter O'Toole in *Lawrence of Arabia*. They greet each other with a customary hand-slap and broad smiles.

'You're looking great, man, but what are you doing here? It's *you* should be baptising me,' says John.

'It's better we do it by the book, Johnny, so that the prophecies will be fulfilled,' says Jesus.

John acknowledges Christ's authority with a nod and, placing his hands on the saviour's head, briefly immerses him in the Jordan, saying, 'I baptise you in the name of your father who art in Heaven.' And as Jesus rises happily to the surface a powerful beam of light cuts through the clouds to illuminate his noble head in a blinding halo of light. Simultaneously a voice booms out from above. 'This is my beloved son in whom I am well pleased.' And at that moment a dove flies down from the clouds and hovers over Christ's head. A gasp from the swelling crowd is followed by a round of applause.

Back in A.R.K. 2001 the creators of this amazing phenomenon smiled gleefully and congratulated themselves.

'Good thinking . . . ' said Mike. 'The dove idea – from now on it will always be associated with love and peace.'

'And the voice was perfect,' enthused Gaby. 'Full of authority, with only an itsy bitsy hint of an Irish accent.'

Mike's head dropped a couple of degrees as he momentarily slipped into modesty mode. Then something on monitor one grabbed his full attention – Gaby's too! A big commotion was going on in the river. The crowd were flocking towards Jesus and the hovering dove while Salome's bodyguards were riding after John who had taken off downriver.

'What now?' yelled Gaby, the pitch of her voice rising a couple of decibels.

'Er, er, er,' replied Mike uncertainly. 'How about a little whiff of Tremazapan gas, knock 'em out for a while?'

Gaby voiced an objection. 'And what if they lose consciousness before they reach the shore?'

'Death by drowning,' said Mike bleakly. Then, more brightly, 'So howsabout we leave them for a while, see what happens. Neither John nor Jesus seems to be in immediate danger and we can always use the stun guns in an emergency.'

'Like now, you mean,' said Gaby. 'Look, they're manhandling John to the shore.'

'No, wait,' said Mike, 'where's Jesus?'

Gaby snapped on the odourometer. 'Safe,' she said, getting a fix on him. 'He's in the crowd there, but not visible.'

'But that goddamn dove is,' said Mike forcefully. 'It's a dead giveaway.'

'Not any more it's not,' said Gaby, taking aim at the bird with her atomiser and reducing it to dust.

'So much for the peace movement,' said Mike as a solitary fluttering feather disappeared from view. 'Now let's put our boys on auto-track.'

'Check,' said Gaby. 'Jesus on monitor one, John on monitor two.'

CHAPTER VII

Enter S.A.T.A.N.

wo days passed and little had happened. John was languishing in a cell in Herod's palace and Jesus was wandering around in the desert, deep in thought.

'He looks as if he's got the cares of the world on his shoulders,' said Gaby.

'He has,' said Mike, 'remember!'

'Do you think he's lost?' said Gaby.

'I don't know, I doubt it,' hazarded Mike. 'He's always got the stars to guide him.'

'It was pretty cloudy last night,' Gaby reminded him.

'So what do you suggest?' asked Mike.

'How about a nice little surprise for him on the other side of that sand dune he's schlepping up right now?' said Gaby.

And with a speed and precision that never failed to surprise her old tin partner, Gaby got to work on the hologram unit and in only a matter of seconds had come up with a solution to help Christ find his way home.

Down below in the white heat of the desert Jesus Christ, near collapse with heatstroke, staggers up yet another of the endless dunes, ever hopeful of a stream or even a mud hole on the far side. No luck, nothing . . . nothing but an undulating sea of glaring sand stretching to the far horizon. Then he notices an object at the foot of the dune which causes his sunburnt brow to furrow. It is a stone. He stumbles down the shifting sands to investigate. He stares at it incredulously for a moment then starts to laugh. The stone is engraved with two arrows pointing in opposite directions and the legend *Jericho ninety-seven miles, Shittim twenty-eight miles.* Christ continues to laugh, he fairly rolls about, and tears would have run down his cheeks had he not been so dehydrated. Red in the face, he goes on laughing until the laugh turns into a dry hacking cough that almost chokes him.

Up above and out of sight his two Guardian Angels were puzzled.

'What's so funny?' mused Gaby.

'Maybe he's flipped,' ventured Mike.

'Maybe the heat's got to him.'

'Maybe an oasis would have been a better idea,' suggested Mike diffidently.

'Oh, God, what I wouldn't give for a sip of water,' whispers Christ aloud through parched lips – as if echoing their thoughts.

If that makes Mike and Gaby sit up – and it does – what happens next makes them almost jump out of their highly polished metal skins. A pool of crystal-clear water slowly materialises at Christ's feet.

'Did you do that?' said Mike and Gaby simultaneously, staring at each other, goggle-eyed. They turn back to the monitor.

As Christ drops to his knees and prepares to plunge his head into the water he suddenly sees a dark shape staring back at him from the mirrored surface. Then, just as if it were a mirage, the shimmering water disappears and Christ finds himself looking at a heap of sand. Slowly he gets to his feet, face to face with – none other than the dark alien.

'Who are you?' says Christ.

'I am the Scientific Aeonistic Technological Angel of Nihilism – Satan for short.'

'What are you doing here?' asks Christ.

'Just keeping an eye open for poor souls lost in the wilderness,' says Satan. 'You'd be surprised what a rich harvest such stony ground yields up.'

'What do you want of me?' asks Christ guardedly.

'I want to help you,' says Satan kindly. 'I come across

your kind every day. You flock here like fleas on a dog's back – mystics, prophets, holy men – all seeing visions, all claiming to be God. I *am* talking to Almighty God, I presume?'

'I am the son of God,' Jesus confirms simply.

'They say God helps those who help themselves,' says Satan. 'Then why not turn this desert into an oasis, turn these stones into bread. It shouldn't be difficult for the son of God.'

'Not difficult, just impossible,' says Gaby, gazing forlornly at monitor one.

'Not for a whiz-kid like you, honey, surely,' says Mike encouragingly.

'Oh, sure I could produce a hologram, no problem, but it wouldn't have any more substance than a mirage.'

'Then how's about a little molecular restructuring on those stones around his feet,' says Mike. 'They won't taste great but at least he won't break his teeth on them.'

'Of course, it's really *us* Satan is tempting, you know that, don't you?' says Gaby. 'It's our technology he's putting to the test.'

'Then turn on the microwave and let's get cooking,' says Mike with an attempt at levity.

Gaby smiles dutifully. 'Roger, all systems on full microbake for his very first miracle, and for Christ's sake let's hope he doesn't get a taste for them.'

'So is the son of God going to turn these stones into crusty bread rolls or is he not?' mocks Satan down below in the desert that simmers as hot as hell.

Jesus runs his dry tongue over his blistered lips and, conscious of the ravening hunger in his empty belly, is sorely tempted, but with a supreme effort puts temptation behind him.

'Man cannot live on bread alone,' he stammers, 'he needs God more.'

'We're off the hook,' exults Gaby, aborting her stones-into-bread programme.

'All our subliminal indoctrination has paid off,' exclaims Mike in jubilation. 'And so long as he truly believes he is the son of God and acts according to the scriptures everything should be hunky dory.'

'But *we* know he's just a regular human being and it seems that Satan's out to prove it.'

'Well, if you won't save yourself maybe you'll show compassion for a friend,' says Satan insinuatingly.

'What's happened to John?' asks Jesus, almost reading Satan's mind. 'Where is he?'

'Enjoying Royal hospitality,' replies Satan cynically. 'In Herod's palace, up to his ankles in shit and chained to a dungeon wall.'

Jesus is alarmed. 'But John is a man of God – a hero of the people. Herod wouldn't dare raise a finger against him no matter how strong his hatred.'

'It's not Herod's hate the Baptist has to fear,' replies Satan, 'but his daughter's lust.'

Christ looks into the bland and impassive eyes of

Satan, which reveal nothing, yet Christ senses he is telling the truth.

'Believe me, only you can save him,' says Satan, placing a claw-like hand on Christ's shoulder, reassuringly. 'Shall we go to the ball, Cinderella?'

Ignoring the mockery Christ gives Satan a terse nod – and the next second they have vanished.

Mike gawped and blinked.

'Out of sight,' said Gaby, gazing blankly at the empty desert.

CHAPTER VIII

Is It a Bird?
Is It a Plane?

hen Christ and Satan materialised inconspicuously in a shadowy corner in the banqueting hall of Herod's palace the place was packed. All the glitterati in Jerusalem were there. Diamonds flashed in the candlelight and rubies glowed like the coals in the giant braziers that stood in each corner of the darkened hall. Saturday nite at the palace was the hottest ticket in town. Herod's balls were legendary. This was not the same Herod who ordered the slaughter of the innocents after the birth of Christ but his lecherous son Antipas, who lolled in gilded splendour between his

adulterous wife Herodias and his jaded mother Jezebel, both wearing crowns like mini chandeliers. And if Jezebel still reminds us of Barbra Streisand on a bad day, Herodias, as she knocks back yet another Harvey Wallbanger, looks a bit like Glenn Close with a hangover. Bleary-eyed, she surveyed her daughter Salome disapprovingly. Proper little cock-teaser, that one. And look at the way Herod lusts after her – making no secret of it either.

'Stop that, Salome, and come over here and sit on my lap,' shouted Herod as he caught sight of yet another flash of pussy. He almost wished it was himself in the cage and not John the Baptist – the cage over which the half-naked Salome was crawling like some sexy bejewelled spider, flashing her fanny inches from the prophet's upturned face as he reviled his tormentor and tugged at the chains that bound him to the bars.

'The time of you and yours is past,' he roared. 'You who have wallowed in depravity and lust shall perish from the Earth.'

'Simmer down, dickhead,' laughed Salome. 'You stink of shit. You should be flattered I even give you the time of day. Your hair is kinda cute though. Of course, it needs a good shampoo and a decent conditioner – just look at all those split ends. Tell you what – why don't we take a shower together? Be kinda fun, don't you think?'

'Child of Sodom, never!' replied John, spitting at her crotch.

'No need for that, Johnny baby,' she admonished

gently, 'I'm wet enough already. Now why don't you get to work with that long tongue of yours? You know you want to . . . ' And she bore down even closer to the iron bars on the top of the cage. By this time Herod was nearly coming in his Y-fronts.

Meanwhile, up in space the two Robots who had picked up Christ again on the odourometer looked on philosophically.

'Who'd have thought women would come to use sex as a weapon?' said Mike.

'I'll tell you one thing,' said Gaby with trepidation.

'What's that?'

'Sure as hell, the shit's gonna hit the fan when she finds out he's a faggot.'

'What's a faggot?' asked Mike, whose vocabulary had more of a scientific bent.

'Faggot, gay, poofter, pansy, queer, nancy boy,' replied Gaby, a note of exasperation edging into her audio-reproductive system.

'Sorry?' apologised Mike, whose word programmer had been more politically correct. 'I still . . . '

'H-O-M-O-S-E-X-U-A-L,' spelt out Gaby, raising her eyes to Heaven.

'Got it,' said Mike with a cheerful nod of comprehension.

Meanwhile the gay prophet is giving the wanton Salome some good advice.

'Seek out the Son of Man, throw yourself at his feet and implore forgiveness.'

'Your tongue, I want to feel your tongue, you self-righteous prick, give it to me.'

'You are cursed, Salome. Flee from the wrath to come.'

'Give it to me and you shall go free.'

'I would rather die first,' says John quietly.

'Give it to me now, d'you hear me?' screams Salome in frustration. 'I command you.'

'And I command you, Salome,' shouts Herod, finally at the end of his tether. 'Desist – you are setting a bad example for our guests.'

'That has to be the understatement of all time,' says Jezebel, glancing at all the fucking guests turned on by her nymphet of a grandchild. Herodias, meanwhile, is less concerned with Salome than with her drooling husband.

'Stop leching after her like that – your own daughter! You disgust me!'

Herod, obsessed with Salome, ignores his wife totally, leaving Jezebel to answer for him.

'You're a fine one to talk – married to poor Archaelus one minute, in bed with his brother the next.'

Tired of this family bickering Herod suddenly snaps.

'Quiet, Mother, or I'll pack you off to the provinces to live with *poor* Archaelus.' Then, returning his attention to Salome, Herod is surprised to find her poised to sit on his lap. Having got nothing but aggro from the prophet Salome is about to get her revenge, though from her innocent demeanour one would never guess it, least of all Herod.

'You called, Daddykins,' she said, smiling sweetly and flopping down on his hard-on with her arms around his neck. Whereupon Herod, highly aroused, starts whispering in her ear.

'What's going on now, do you suppose?' asked Mike, mesmerised by this Royal soap opera.

'Buggered if I know,' said Gaby. 'But as sure as hell they're not discussing the weather. I'd say he was propositioning her.'

'Try boosting the sound level,' suggested Mike.

'Check,' said Gaby, 'but there's a heck of a lot of background noise to contend with.'

She was right – the grunts of the male guests grinding away, mingled with the simulated groans of their partners (of both sexes) all but drowned the subdued whisperings of the incestuous couple on the throne.

'Strip for me, sweetie, and I'll give you the Earth,' promised Herod.

'You're an old fibber, Daddykins,' chided Salome. 'You don't own the Earth, Caesar does and what's more, Caesar owns you.'

'You've been listening to Granny again,' growled Herod. 'What do you want then? How about a trip up the Nile on the Royal barge?'

'That would be nice . . . ' said Salome, giving Herod cause for hope, 'once the air conditioning's fixed.'

Desperate, Herod tried again. 'Please, Salome, please, I'll give you half my Kingdom.'

'Try being more specific, Dad,' said Salome.

'Then how about two tickets for *Cats* at the Colosseum – they're like gold dust.'

'Seeing a bunch of ancient Brits being thrown to the lions doesn't turn me on, Dad.'

'Then how about a bejewelled vibrator . . . and your own credit card?' he added in desperation.

'You don't have to bribe me to dance for you, Pop, 'specially when you're pissed. It will be my pleasure . . .' she crooned, ' . . . though there is one little thing I'd like . . . But it's so insignificant it's hardly worth mentioning.'

'Then don't mention it, take it, you shall have it,' cried Herod magnanimously.

'Promise?' wheedled Salome with a provocative wriggle of her ass.

'Promise,' said Herod, holding back orgasm only by calling to mind sex with his wife.

Then Salome slid with agonising slowness off his lap and with a clap of her hands – to activate the court musicians – went into her dance . . . if you could call it that. For as the band swung into a Middle-Eastern version of 'The Stripper' she simply revolved on the spot and after each seventh turn dropped an article of clothing. And whereas her cavorting on the cage of the holy man had been a king-sized turn-on this was just a naughty child winding up a horny parent. But it was novel, intriguing. The general fornication ground to a halt as the guests began getting more kicks out of Herod's chagrin than shagging their partners. Shit! A five-year-old could do better than that. And the more garments Salome threw at Herod's bunion-covered feet the more like a little child she became and the more like a voyeuristic paedophile he became – and he knew it – everyone knew it and relished it, till with a final fling of her bejewelled and padded bra at his head Salome stamped her bare little foot and flaunted her bare little chest for all to see. Except that everyone was looking at Herod and laughing fit to bust at the sight of the mighty monarch sitting there with egg on his face and Salome's glittering bra dangling over his head like a couple of oversize earrings. But Herod was not amused and the mirth died into silence as he glowered around the hall and everyone wondered what next. They did not have long to wait.

'Can I have my present now please, Daddy?' said Salome with child-like candour.

'What is it?' growled Herod, turning deep purple.

The crowd waited. They almost expected her to ask for a lollipop or a fluffy white rabbit . . . until she turned to John the Baptist with a sneer and drew a deep breath. The ensuing silence, which seemed like an eternity, was broken by a sudden and very audible *CLICK!* It came from the deserted corner of the hall in which the two interlopers still lurked in the shadows and was caused by Satan pressing a silver button on the top of an ebony staff clasped in his black talons. Instantly everyone except Satan and Jesus, standing at his side, who were outside the orbit of power transmitted by the staff, appeared to become thinner and almost frozen in time.

'You have turned them to stone,' said Jesus, marvelling at Satan's power. 'It's a miracle.'

Satan chuckled. 'I leave miracles to the likes of grubby little Gods like you. This is pure science.'

'But you have made time stand still,' said Christ in awe.

'You flatter me, but as yet that is still even beyond *my* capabilities – as yet the tachyon interactor hasn't the power to stop it. No, I've merely dilated their time. And if you look really carefully you'll see that everything is actually moving in super slow motion. So you've only a brief moment to intervene.'

'What do you mean?' asked Christ.

'Dear me, you are the innocent one,' said Satan with undisguised irritation. 'I should have thought it was obvious. Observe the way Salome is looking at John . . .'

Christ did so and saw the venom in her eyes. 'Like a cobra about to strike,' he whispered.

'And it is within your power to change her mind . . .' hissed Satan, 'if you really are the son of God.'

Up in the clouds Mike and Gaby stared glumly at monitor one.

'Still playing games, I see,' mused Gaby.

'With us as the unwilling contestants,' replied Mike.

'What are our chances?' asked Gaby.

'Well, if Christ calls on God to intervene and we fail him he'll lose faith in his own divinity.'

'In which case we've blown it,' said Gaby.

'Let's hope he remembers what Moses used to tell the Jews whenever they were up shit creek without a paddle,' said Mike.

'Refresh my memory bank,' said Gaby.

'It's God's will,' grinned Mike.

'Yes, of course, God's will, God's will,' laughed Gaby. 'Yeah, that takes care of everything. Let's zap him with a quick reminder,' and she immediately set about activating the transmitter aimed directly at the memory chip lodged in the Messiah's brain. 'Hit it, Mike, hit it. She's about to gab.'

'Time's up,' whispered Satan in Christ's ear. 'Your pal is just about to be decapitated.'

Torn by conflicting emotions Christ watched, fascinated, as Salome's mouth slowly but remorselessly opened to draw in the breath that would seal the Baptist's fate.

'God swill, God swill, God swill,' gabbled Mike.

'God's will, God's will,' spouted Gaby over his shoulder.

'Hey, what's up?' said Mike heatedly.

'You said "God swill",' explained Gaby, 'you're confusing him.'

But if Christ was confused he didn't look it, he just looked ineffably weary as if there had been a great conflict raging within him.

'What is foretold in the scriptures must come to pass,' he said. 'It is God's will.'

'I guessed you'd chicken out,' smiled Satan, releasing the time dilation with a gesture of triumph.

'. . . The head of John the Baptist,' laughed Salome, beaming around the hall as if she'd said something really clever.

Everyone, especially Herod, thought they hadn't heard right or she'd got it wrong. Everyone that is except

Satan and Jesus who dropped his head and murmured,
'May God have mercy on his soul.'

'What did you say, child?' asked Herod incredulously.

'You know exactly what I said,' replied Salome, suddenly turning into a hard-faced bitch. 'And I want it now.'
And once more she stamped her little foot – and it was
heard throughout the hall.

'All right! You've had your little joke, and you're the
centre of attention once again which is how you like it.
Now grow up for God's sake and ask for something
sensible.'

'Give me the head of John the Baptist,' she repeated
stubbornly.

'Nothing changes,' croaked Jezebel out of the blue.
'She always pulled the heads off her dolls. For God's sake
give her what she wants, son, or we'll never hear the
end of it.'

'And just how long are you going to put up with that
man's insults?' said Herodias as John began cursing them
again and Salome kept repeating, 'Gimme, gimme,
gimme.' This together with the expectant babbling of
the crowd soon became a sheer cacophony . . .

. . . until Mike gave Gaby the nod to kill the sound. Dead
silence followed as the Robots watched Salome jump on
top of the Prophet's cage and grab ahold of his hair,
nearly pulling it out by the roots, while Herod gave the
signal for the Royal executioner, a negro giant dressed in
the skins of his many victims, to saw through the
Prophet's neck with a blunt scimitar. Blood spurted all
over Salome's crotch as the dying man screamed a silent

scream that sent shudders down the Robots' spines, activated by their finely tuned Yukometers. Then as Salome pulled the bloody head, still cursing, through the bars and sat on it, Mike killed the picture too. It was all a little too much for these sensitive souls who lived by a strict code of ethics. How they wished they could have erased their memory banks. But duty called.

'Do you think they've cleared up the mess yet?' asked Gaby.

'Let's take a peep,' said Mike, reactivating sound and picture on monitor one. Nothing! The hall was empty. Even the blood was gone.

'Holy Moses, where's the Messiah?' said Mike.

'Search me, but we'll soon find out,' said Gaby, punching in Christ's odourspot number. What happened next had them goggle-eyed: according to the odourometer Christ was fifteen thousand miles due west of where he had been five minutes earlier, and even stranger was the fact that although the odourometer was accurate to .0 of an inch there was no sign of him on the monitor – and, equally significantly, there was no sign of Satan either.

'Where the hell have they gone?' queried Gaby.

'Search me,' said Mike. 'Check for malfunction.'

'Check,' said Gaby.

'Double check,' said Mike.

'Check,' said Gaby.

Nothing. The picture – of a grassy, boulder-strewn landscape with a scattering of deciduous trees remained stubbornly unchanged, as did the orange spot bang in the middle of the screen, representing Christ.

'Notice anything strange?' asked Mike.

'Well, according to the altimeter he's exactly one thousand four hundred and fifty-three feet above sea level and yet there is no sign of a hill.'

'Which can mean only one thing,' said Mike, looking Gaby straight in the eye to see if she'd caught on. She had.

'They've gone into the future!' she exclaimed brightly.

'Maybe there was an earthquake and they're standing on a mountain peak or on top of a pyramid,' suggested Mike.

'Well, there's only one way to find out,' said Gaby, switching the time machine to standby.

'Go easy,' cautioned Mike, 'the last time we used that we had to shut down for a year.'

'I know,' Gaby concurred. 'It eats up energy faster than a black hole swallows galaxies. Rossum's working on it but is having problems with his theory of relativity.'

'Well, who knows,' Mike said, 'maybe one of these days human knowledge might catch up to our level and give him a helping hand.'

'Fat chance,' said Gaby, locking herself into time-warp mode.

'Well, if they don't catch us up and eventually surpass us we're doomed,' said Mike.

Gaby did not respond and for good reason. And for the benefit of readers with Alzheimer's disease it might be time to remind them that the sole reason Rossum started the human race was in the hope that someone would eventually invent an antidote to the disease that threatened to wipe the Robots out – an antidote that had so far eluded every computer in the Rossum solar system – an antidote to metal erosion, or good old-fashioned *rust**, as it is more commonly known.

So, mindful of their purpose, our two metallic friends renewed their efforts to find the Saviour.

'I'll cruise ahead a decade at a time till we catch them up,' said Gaby. 'It's locking in that does the most damage.'

'Maybe we should wait till they come back,' said Mike, sounding a note of caution.

'Maybe they never will,' said Gaby, switching on the ignition.

And they both eagerly watched the monitor and the ever-changing seasons that flowed rapidly across the screen. Trees grew and died and herds of hulking great animals appeared munching the grass.

'Buffalo seem to be breeding nicely,' remarked Gaby nonchalantly.

'When was it we introduced them to the Americas?'

'Not long ago,' said Gaby. 'Can't be more than 25,000 Earth years. I wonder why they've developed that hump?'

'Holy Rossum!' they both exclaimed in unison as they saw red men on horseback pumping the poor creatures full of arrows so that they resembled a lot of stampeding pin-cushions.

'There's your answer,' exclaimed Mike. 'Now what?'

---

*Plastic was, as yet, unknown to them. Even their credit cards were made of metal.

And they watched in silence as a speeded-up sailing ship appeared on the scene, disgorging a bevy of pantalooned men in pork-pie hats. It was at this very moment that the time machine began slowing down. Simultaneously sound and image began to break up and the spaceship juddered as it fast approached the time barrier.

'We the Pilgrim Fathers thank . . . od . . . or a safe passage and name . . . ace . . . Manhat . . . n I'land . . . '

This was followed by a small explosion and a puff of smoke which sent the spaceship into a spin as whistles blew, bells rang and lights flashed.

'We've had it,' said Mike. Gaby didn't answer, she was too dizzy to speak.

If only our time travellers had enjoyed the technology available to Satan they could have moved on those necessary two hundred and seventy eight years since that historic day the Pilgrim Fathers landed on Plymouth Rock to present-day New York City and seen Satan and Jesus balancing precariously on top of the Empire State Building.

'Follow me,' says Satan, 'and not only will the present be yours but also the future. I am the all powerful, I am science, your God is fiction. Your God never was and never will be.'

Jesus feels a sudden pang of fear and prays for time.

'God is Alpha and Omega,' says Jesus. 'He always was and ever shall be.'

'Afraid of falling?' says Satan, fully aware of Christ's sense of vertigo. 'Surely if you are truly the son of God he will send a host of angels to raise you up before you hit the sidewalk.'

Feeling alone and abandoned, Christ can only quote scriptures and hope for the best.

'It is written that you shall not tempt the Lord thy God.'

'Says who?' laughs Satan and gives Jesus an almighty shove that sends him hurtling down towards Fifth Avenue over a thousand feet below and the growing crowd gaping up at him. Then, a split second before Christ is about to hit the kerb and end up like redcurrant jelly, a streak of blue, red and yellow appears out of the sky from nowhere and scoops Jesus into its arms and up, up and away into the realms of invisibility. Whereupon the crowd blink, laugh, applaud and go about their business, imagining they have just been witness to a clever stunt from their favourite TV show – *Superman.*

CHAPTER IX

Dinner at the King David

econds after Christ disappeared into the mild blue yonder Mike manhandled the stick-shift of the time module back into neutral and for several minutes the ship was stuck in time – like a needle in a damaged groove of an old black disc repeating the same signal over and over. In this case causing the Pilgrim Fathers to continuously repeat Amen and put on their hats, only to appear bare-headed with hands clasped in prayer a moment later.

Then with a clunk and a grating of gears Mike managed to get the ship into reverse and smiled to himself as he watched the monitor screen where everything whizzed backwards – with arrows springing out of the backs of the buffalo and returning to the quivers of the hunters via their bows as they, too, galloped backwards, swallowing their wild whoops and yells as they went. Then, as Mike reversed and set course for the Holy Land once more, everything became a blur until the present returned with a bump and time began creeping forward second by second as per usual. And it was the bump that put Gaby to rights and reactivated the gyrotop that maintained her equilibrium.

'Where are we?' she asked.

'Back in Jerusalem on standard time,' said Mike. Then Gaby remembered their mission.

'Christ, where is he?' she suddenly exclaimed.

'I was just about to programme his odourspot number,' said Mike. 'How're you feeling?'

'I've got a splitting headache,' moaned Gaby. 'Time travel doesn't agree with me.'

'Take a couple of aspirins with a dose of three-in-one,' advised Mike. 'I swear by it.'

'I prefer herbal remedies,' said Gaby, helping herself to a shot of date oil.

'Well, so far there's no sign of him, the odourometer only registers one of his smocks hanging in the closet at home.'

'Maybe we should hang around,' suggested Gaby, 'he must be getting peckish after forty days and forty nights in the wilderness without a bite to eat.'

'And not a shekel in his pocket,' added Mike. So without further discussion they tuned into the home of the holy family.

*

Hollow-eyed and drawn, Mary sat on the sofa with her feet up flicking idly through a fashion magazine while Joe put the finishing touches to a pin table he was making for an amusement arcade and burnt the cheese blintzs he was cooking at the same time.

'Honey, I don't like to interfere,' said Mary cautiously, 'but something tells me those blintzs are just about ready.'

'Holy Mary, Mother of God, so they are,' Joe exclaimed, and with a bound to the stove he scooped up the pan and stared guiltily at the burnt offerings.

'Tomorrow, *I'll* do the cooking. I feel much better today,' lied Mary.

'Now take it easy and quit worrying,' admonished Joseph. 'You've worn yourself to a shadow looking for him and fretting isn't going to bring him back any quicker. He's not a kid any more. He's a grown man, he can take care of himself.'

'Joe can't fool me,' said Gaby, high in the sky. 'He's as worried as she is.'

'And I'm more worried than the both of them together,' added Mike.

'Now, will you all quit worrying,' said the voice of Christ, out of the blue. 'I'm home safe and sound.'

And the Robots watched with astonishment as Jesus gave Joe a big hug and kissed Mary full on the mouth – a big, lingering kiss that acted on her like the kiss of life. Pale and wan one minute, rosy-cheeked and vibrant the next. It was a minor miracle.

'Now, hurry along and hop into your best bib and tucker, folks – I've booked us into the King David for dinner.'

'But your mother's been poorly, son,' stammered Joseph.

'Poorly?' laughed Jesus. 'She's a picture of health – look at her.' And they all did and Jesus was right, there was no denying it. Mary looked as young as a girl. 'Quick, Mom, get into your glad rags,' urged Jesus. 'They can't hold the reservation beyond eight-thirty.'

'But the King David is expensive,' said Mary. 'Why, the cover charge alone would keep us in goat burgers for a month.'

'Quit worrying, Mom,' chided Jesus. 'The Lord will provide.'

Mike and Gaby looked at each other in disbelief.

'His faith in God is quite touching,' said Mike.

'He really has some nerve, this guy,' exclaimed Gaby. 'What does he expect us to do, rob a bank?'

'Search me,' said Mike, 'but talking of robbery we could always teleport a few thousand shekels from the Temple to his back pocket. Those bureau de change shysters would soon make it up again.'

'No problem,' said Gaby, putting Mike's plan into operation, 'but let's hope he doesn't make a habit of it.'

'A habit of eating in expensive restaurants, you mean,' said Mike. 'Surely after all that fasting in the wilderness you don't begrudge him a square meal with his folks.'

'But what if it doesn't stop there?' said Gaby. 'What if

he decides to treat every bum in Jerusalem to open house at the King David?'

'No chance,' said Mike breezily. 'They have a strict dress code at the King David, those bums would never make it past the doorman.'

Silently they watched the monitor, keeping their thoughts to themselves. Sometimes Mike could be a bit brusque with Gaby.

Meanwhile the holy family, in high spirits, were still catching up on all the news as they tucked into their nosh at the trendiest restaurant in town.

'Your mother thought you'd been arrested along with Johnny and got the chop,' said Joe.

'I feel real bad about Johnny,' said Jesus sadly. 'I was there, I saw it all . . . yet I didn't lift a finger to help him.'

Mary took her boy's hand in her own. 'Don't reproach yourself, Jesu, what could you have done? They'd have cut you down, too, and there would have been two deaths in the family. It was God's will.'

'That's what I told myself, Mother. But to tell you the truth, I was scared shitless.'

'And I'd have felt the same if I'd been in your shoes,' said Joe supportively. 'Who wouldn't?'

'I don't know,' said Jesus, 'but if there *are* any brave souls out there I'm going to find them, or die in the attempt.'

Not surprisingly, perhaps, a silence followed.

'Does that mean you'll be leaving us again?' asked Mary, voicing their thoughts.

'Tomorrow at first light,' said Jesus simply.

'So soon?' said Mary. 'We'll be up all night packing.'

'Oh, no we won't,' said Jesus, squeezing Mary's hand. 'I shall leave as I came.'

'Then you must take a packed lunch,' insisted Mary. 'We've still got all your favourite things there in the larder – unless Joe's finished them all up. Have you, Joe?'

'No, of course not, Mary,' he replied, flustered. 'The only thing we're fresh out of is chunky peanut butter but there's a whole jar of smooth left.'

'But you know full well he can't stand the smooth variety,' said Mary.

'Look, Mom,' said Jesus, 'when I hit the road I'm going to travel light. So don't concern yourself with what I'll eat or what I'll wear.'

Mary took in her son's words but was still unable to shake off a mother's concern. Christ tried another tack, one he was destined to use with increasing frequency. 'Look, Mom, do you remember those birds we used to see in the desert? They never had a larder, did they? Or call to mind those fabulous lilies down by the river, dancing in the breeze. Compared with them Solomon in all his glory looked like a bum on welfare. So if God can take care of tweety-pies and wild flowers, I guess he can afford a handout for his only begotten son once in a while.'

'Let me come with you for company,' pleaded Mary.

'I appreciate that, Mom, I really do, but your place is here with Joe,' said Jesus, glancing kindly at his step-father who was engrossed in the floor show. 'And don't worry about me, I won't be lonely. From tomorrow the whole world will be my family.'

'What do you make of that?' said Mike to Gaby.

'Well, as drag-acts go I've certainly seen worse,' she replied.

'Not the floor show,' snapped Mike. 'I meant the Messiah's trip.'

'Well, he seems all set and rarin' to go, and with our backup he's got all the makings of a swell mouthpiece,' enthused Gaby.

'He seems to have the makings of a faith-healer as well,' said Mike. 'And that's gotta be a bonus, too.'

'You mean the miracle cure he worked on Mary,' said Gaby. 'I wouldn't set too much store by that. I'd say her condition was psychosomatic. Jesu's disappearance was the cause of her decline and his reappearance was the cure.'

'Even so,' said Mike, 'we shouldn't underestimate his powers, and he has amazing self-confidence.'

'Thinking yourself to be the son of God must help a little,' said Gaby, yawning. 'I don't know about you but I could use a little shut-eye, it's been a hard day's flight.'

'Me too,' said Mike. 'And I have a hunch we've got another tough day ahead of us, so slap her on auto and let's have ourselves a little dream time.'

'Roger,' said Gaby, pulling the stick-shift that would send them shooting towards the sandman in the Land of Nod.

CHAPTER X

Stoned

hen Mike and Gaby, having serviced both themselves and the ship, picked up Jesus on the odourometer the next day he was running – yes, actually running. Does that surprise you? Think about it. You've probably yawned your way through at least one Biblical epic in your lifetime, so cast your mind back – did you ever see the Messiah move even as fast as a model on a catwalk? No siree, you did not. True, it is not easy to run in a floor-length frock, and to pull your frock above your knees in order to run without falling flat on your face would be considered by Hollywood to be undignified.

But the Messiah wasn't concerned in the least with his image according to Hollywood as he belted along the beach towards the fracas taking place on the edge of the small fishing village he was rapidly approaching at a healthy 15 m.p.h. And as every pace brought him closer so the confusion began to clarify.

Egged on by a group of priests an angry crowd are stoning a young woman – or attempting to, for between the mob and their victim are two men wielding a fishing net with all the dexterity of gladiators. But despite their valiant efforts they are outflanked . . . and unable to stop a stone the size of a baseball *pow*ing towards the woman's tearful face. But Jesus *can* and fields it brilliantly before returning it to sender, knocking off his pompous priestly hat in the process. Stunned silence followed by laughter from the crowd accompanies the chief priest's humiliation, though one or two giggle nervously. It is a punishable offence to attack a priest. But so audacious is the Messiah's behaviour that the chief priest finds himself stammering a reply.

'She's an adulteress, she must be punished according to the law of the scriptures.'

'That law's old hat,' shouted the bigger of the two fishermen, whose name was Peter.

'That law is as old as the ark,' yelled his brother Andrew. 'It's antideluvian.'

This was above the heads of most of the villagers who were growing impatient to resume their favourite sport, second only in popularity to baiting blind beggars.

'Stone her, she's a trollop,' shouted one . . . 'A whore, a slut, a wanton, a tramp, a tart,' screamed others, casting about them for more rocks to throw. Surrounded, Christ took the woman in his arms and did his best to protect her.

Meanwhile Mike and Gaby were preparing for the impending onslaught.

'Set the CO_2 laser to autolock – max output,' ordered Mike. And as Gaby's hands blurred across the instrument panel a laser-wave oscillogram appeared on monitor two while a cross on monitor one tracked every flying object coming within the vicinity of Christ and the woman, vaporising them in a puff of smoke with the oscillating laser beam. Whereupon the hail of stones dwindled to a trickle as the crowd began to wonder. Only the priests continued the barrage and fortunately their aim was poor. Fortunately, because the Robots' missile-destruct system was gradually being phased out by an even stronger signal from an outside force.

'It's synthesising our laser frequency with equal amplitude and phase reversal,' observed Mike.

'Watch this,' said Gaby, hitting a touch sensor. 'I've shifted the frequency.'

'No good,' said Mike, 'the jammer's phase is locked on; track down the source of interference on another channel.'

In a flash Gaby did so. 'It's coming from inside that building on the corner. I'll get an exact fix on it . . . Shit!' Without warning all the monitors blacked out and filled with white noise.

'We've been shut down,' continued Gaby angrily as all

the lights went out. 'It's these fucking powers of darkness again.'

'Jesus, you're on your own,' said Mike mournfully.

Having collected a fresh supply of stones the mob are ready to renew the attack on the woman, but hesitate for fear of hitting the stranger protecting her.

'Stand aside,' says the chief priest, intimidated by the Messiah's fearless stance of authority. 'We have no quarrel with you. This woman is guilty of adultery and must be punished by stoning, according to the law.'

'Very well,' says Christ, stepping away from the miserable woman. 'Go right ahead and let the bestest person here have the honour of throwing the first stone.' Confusion reigns. The villagers, a shifty lot only too aware of each other's shortcomings, look to the priests to set an example.

Momentarily intimidated, the chief priest resorts to ranting instead of rocks. 'You defy the Commandments of Moses!'

'And *you* defy the Commandment of God: you shall not kill,' replies Jesus firmly. 'Wipe the crap from your own eyes before you look for the speck of dirt in hers.' The priests are speechless, the crowd delighted. This is the language they understand – all that talk of Moses left them cold. Jesus presses home his advantage. 'And don't let's be slaves to the letter of the law, let's go for its true spirit. It's dead easy to victimise a young chick caught with her knickers down, but I reckon that any horny dude who even fancies a bit of crumpet has committed adultery in his head. And the same goes for you women as well.'

'Hey, go easy, buster, or you'll put me outa business. You're slagging off my clientele.'

All turn towards the interruption coming from the balcony of the cat house on the corner where the jamming device is situated. The speaker is Mary Magdalene, the village madam, known far and wide as M.M., the original tart with a heart of gold. And those of you who remember Mae West in *Diamond Lil* will have a fair picture of her in your mind . . . right from the bedroom eyes down to the seductive sway of her hips. She looks down at Jesus and smiles, more sexy than censorious, and then addresses the onlookers.

'From where I'm standing I can see at least three unpaid bills.' She pauses to allow more than one customer to examine both his memory and his conscience. And more than one customer begins to melt away. 'That's it,' M.M. declaims, 'clear off back to your wives before I start naming names . . . like Ezekiel the priest, here . . . ' and she points accusingly at the chief priest who starts to cringe ' . . . He spends a lot of time on his knees but it's not spent in prayer.' She gives another infectious laugh, causing most of the locals to join in. Humiliated, Ezekiel skulks off with his fellow priests, harbouring resentment and plans for revenge, while the remainder of the villagers drift away in groups of two and three, glancing from time to time at Jesus and the distressed woman cradled protectively in his arms.

'Don't cry, it's all right,' says Jesus reassuringly. 'Tell me, do you love your husband?'

Between deep sobs the woman replies, 'He loves, he says he loves . . . to beat the shit out of me.'

'And your lover . . . tell me about him.'

The woman hesitates. Jesus takes her hand, holds it reassuringly. 'He kisses away the pain,' she replies, 'he comforts me.'

Jesus kisses her gently on both cheeks and says, 'Take care, love, and God be with you.'

Heartened, the woman returns his look, seeming to gather strength with each new breath.

'Hey, you two,' shouts M.M., 'break it up or people will talk. Bring her inside, buster, so she can rest up. And Pete and Andy . . . the drinks are on the house. Come on in and bring your mates. The rest of you . . . fuck off home and leave us in peace, you'll give the neighbourhood a bad name.'

And as the baddies broke it up and the goodies made their way to the brothel Mike and Gaby gave a start as the monitor screens zazzed abruptly to life again, albeit out of lock.

'Quick, adjust the line hold,' said Mike.

'Check,' said Gaby, flicking a switch that restored the picture once more. 'Why d'ya think the interference just cut out like that?'

'Because the jamming signal in the brothel has been switched off – either to conserve energy or because we've shut down our laser unit.'

'Seems like Satan's at work again,' said Gaby. 'Let's take a peek inside and see if we can trace him.'

CHAPTER XI

Miracle in the Cat House

nside the brothel visibility is down to a couple of yards as most every-one around is smoking pot.

'Here, have a drag,' says M.M., passing the distressed woman a joint. 'What's your name, honey?'

'Ruth,' replies the girl, taking a drag.

'Then take it easy, Ruth, we'll look after you,' says M.M., turning to one of her girls. 'Lilian, this is Ruth. She'll be resting up here a while; give her a hot bath and find her somewhere to sleep.' And with Ruth taken care of she switches her attention to Jesus. 'What'll it be, buster, name your poison.'

'I'd love a cool draught of Adam's wine,' says Jesus, much to M.M.'s surprise.

'Water!' she exclaims. 'We only use water for washing off or washing up. The water around here's poisonous. Even the camels won't touch it. But if you're on the wagon or T.T. why not have a passion-fruit cordial, put you in the mood for a little nooky if you're so inclined?'

Jesus smiles and says, 'How would you rate the wine here?'

M.M. smiles back and says, 'The opposite of this house – quite respectable.'

'Then I'll gladly try some,' says Jesus.

'Well said,' enthuses M.M. 'And I shall join you myself. Naomi,' she calls to a passing redhead, 'two glasses of the Premier Cru for me and my guest.'

The poor redhead looks abashed. 'Sorry, M.M., we're fresh out of stock, I was just gonna break the bad news.'

'So early in the day?' exclaims M.M.

'Well, you did say that everyone should drink your health,' the girl replies.

'Thank God I only have one birthday a year,' says M.M. 'Any more and I'd go bankrupt. Now the gentleman'll think me inhospitable.'

'Not at all,' laughs Jesus. 'What's your favourite tipple?'

'Well, I wouldn't say no to a virile young Samarian,' says M.M. 'Why?'

'To those who give shall be given,' says Jesus.

'Give over,' says M.M. 'The only karma I believe in's the Karma Sutra.'

Jesus chuckles and catches the eye of an old woman with a withered hand filling some finger bowls with water from a large clay jar. 'Recharge their glasses, good mother,' says Jesus, 'the drinks are on me.'

'I feel another miracle coming on,' said Gaby without much enthusiasm. 'Are there enough constituents to synthesise the wine locally?'

'Well,' said Mike, considering, 'there's water, hydrogen and plenty of carbon dioxide, due to those breaking wind, though we're pretty low on phosphorus. But I think we should be able to transmute the water – unless Satan decides otherwise, that is.'

'He may be afraid to show his hand again so soon,' said Gaby. 'And who knows, he could be curious to see if we can pull it off. But what are we going to do about the lack of phosphorus?'

'Since it's a single pure element we should be able to send its spectral-emission energy to the water jar,' said Mike.

'Then let's give it a whirl,' said Gaby, flashing up the spectral emission of phosphorus on a screen. And after just a second or so of fancy finger-work Gaby was able to report, 'Quark reorientation process complete, wave form reconstructed and transmitted. There!'

'Well done. I wonder what Satan will make of that,' smiled Mike.

'It was nothing,' demurred Gaby, 'just a simple exercise in elementary physics.'

'Don't sell yourself short,' said Mike with an admiring look that suffused Gaby's body with a warm rosy glow.

Then, like two children who had planned a big surprise
for their friends, they turned their attention back to the
brothel where Martha was about to pour Jesus . . . a
refreshing draught of an exceedingly young Samarian.

'Happy birthday,' says Jesus, raising his glass to M.M.
before downing it in a couple of gulps. 'Mmm, quite
passable for a local plonk,' continues Jesus, signalling to
Martha for a refill. 'Why not join me in a glass?' he asks
the madam.

M.M. gives a knowing chuckle. 'I guessed you were a
magician from the start; so thanks but no thanks,
coloured water does nothing for me.'

'Then I trust you won't object to your servants joining
me in drinking your health.'

'Why not?' said M.M., laughing. 'Everyone else has.
They drink coloured water all the time with the customers, anyway.' And she gives a wink of approval to old
Martha who refills Christ's glass then pours drinks for
herself and Naomi. Smiling nervously the women raise
their goblets to join Jesus in a toast.

'Blessed are the pure in heart, for they shall see God.'

'That lets me out, then,' says M.M., passing off her
embarrassment in a quip as the others sip their drinks
and stare at Jesus in wonder.

'Come on, girls,' chides M.M. 'Act drunk like you do
with the customers.'

Unsure about how to react the women play dumb.
Nobody contradicts M.M.! Sensing something is up,
M.M. takes a swig herself and with a smile of approval,
another, and another.

'Right,' she says, beaming at Jesus and pointing to a row of jars on a shelf, 'I'll take as many as you can deliver, two hundred drachmas each. What do you say?'

"Make it three hundred,' says Jesus, smiling.

'Two-fifty,' says M.M.

'You've got yourself a deal,' says Jesus.

They shake on it and M.M. turns to Naomi. 'Fetch over a jar, sweetie, and this time don't let him near it.'

By now everyone in the room has gathered around to join in the fun.

'OK, boys, you be the judge and if he's pulled a fast one and it's not up to snuff, Heaven help him.'

And as the crowd jostle with their goblets outstretched to Naomi Jesus turns his eyes Heavenward with an enigmatic smile.

'You know, at times I almost get the feeling he's on to us and wonder just who's manipulating who,' said Gaby.

'And for my next trick,' said Mike with a flourish, 'what shall it be? A rabbit out of a hat or find the lady?'

'Search me,' replied Gaby, 'but I've a hunch we're just about to find out. Get a load of Martha.'

Mike focused his attention on the old woman with the withered hand who had abandoned her jar and was crawling on all fours through the carousing crowd towards the Messiah, who was being congratulated on all sides.

'Ten to one she's after a miracle cure,' predicted Mike.

'No takers,' said Gaby. 'Let's just hope we can handle it.'

And they watched intently as Martha made her way beneath the protection of a stout table, her crippled hand reaching out ever closer to Christ.

A hand appeared as an X-ray image on monitor four in the spaceship. 'Well, at least her bone structure isn't deformed,' observed Mike with some relief. 'But the muscles seem to be in a state of permanent contraction.'

'Maybe something is inhibiting the nerve impulses from reaching her finger muscles,' suggested Gaby.

'Spot on,' enthused Mike. 'A quick computer thermographic lepton analysis should diagnose the malfunction pronto.'

And in a flash there appeared on monitor five varicoloured contours of Martha's hand, colours which Mike programmed and analysed on monitor six.

'I guessed as much,' remarked Gaby, looking at the word 'syphilis' flashing on the screen. 'Do we have an antidote?'

'No problem,' said Mike, checking a computer readout. 'Curareic Synapseine . . . Teleporting on contact.'

And as Martha's deformed hand touches Christ's robe Mike hits a sensor which instantly transmits the high-energy curative beam of chemical particles. *Pow!* Martha curls into a ball under the table and hides her 'cured' hand in the folds of her dress, while way above her the Robots grin and give each other the thumbs-up sign.

But down below nobody in the room has witnessed the 'miracle', although Jesus is suddenly aware that something supernatural has happened.

'Who touched me? Someone touched me.'

M.M., sharp-eyed and habitually suspicious, catches sight of Martha under the table, hiding her hand.

'Martha, what are you up to? Is that the way to repay the gentleman – picking his pocket?'

'Leave her alone,' Jesus interjects.

But M.M. is in full flight and convinced of Martha's guilt.

'For a cripple you've got mighty nimble fingers. Show me what you're hiding.'

And she grabs hold of Martha, who is weeping now, drags her from beneath the table and raises her clasped hand in the air for all to see. And what they see astonishes them – as Martha's once-crippled hand opens of its own accord. Most of the onlookers know Martha well and can hardly believe their eyes. Water into wine is one thing, but this is something else and the thought that is beginning to form in most of the onlookers' minds is finally put into words by Peter, the big fisherman. 'A miracle!'

Whereupon a silence falls over the entire room in marked contrast to the hilarity in the spaceship where the two Robots are cracking up.

'This is great,' chortles Mike. 'This is terrific.'

'This is the start of something big,' responds Gaby excitedly.

Meanwhile Jesus, realising what has happened, turns to the trembling Martha who still holds her newborn hand wonderingly in the air, although the stunned M.M. has dropped it like a hot potato.

'Why did you touch me, Martha?' asks Jesus kindly.

Martha hesitates, knowing all eyes are on her, before replying in a firm voice, 'I knew you could heal me.'

Everyone – the customers, the two fishermen, the girls, the priests (who have crept in to spy) and even the odd man out, a Roman Centurion, breathlessly await Christ's reaction.

'Your faith has cured you,' says Jesus, gently taking Martha's hand and kissing it. 'Your sins are forgiven.'

Silence again as everyone tries to sort out the meaning of Christ's words. A silence that is broken by the chief priest Ezekiel, bent on revenge. 'Look at him, the drunken blasphemer, sitting in a brothel with whores and thieves, forgiving sins, mocking God; who do . . . '

Christ jumps up in anger, cutting him off. 'Are you blind? Are you going to turn your back on the truth for ever? When John was among you, he fasted and abstained and you called him a lunatic and betrayed him. And now you accuse me of whoring and blasphemy. You hear but you never understand, see but never perceive, for your hearts are made of stone, your ears are deaf and your eyes blind. You turn your back on the truth.'

'And you who speak arrogantly of John the Baptist, take care you don't share his fate,' says Ezekiel.

'John was a truly humble servant of God,' replies Jesus. 'To share his martyrdom would be an honour.'

'The only true servants of God are we Pharisees,' says Ezekiel. 'Shining monuments to the Law of Moses.'

'Whitewashed tombs are shining monuments too – on the outside,' says Jesus, 'but inside they are full of stinking corruption.'

'How dare you mock those whom even Herod himself has called "the salt of the earth"?' hisses a spidery priest standing next to Ezekiel.

'Salt that has passed its sell-by date and lost its flavour,' replies Jesus contemptuously, 'and has been dumped in the gutter.'

'That's good enough for me,' says M.M. 'I don't want your kind in here any more.' And she turns to her brother, a seven-foot giant knocking back a jar of wine single-handed. 'Lazarus, throw these whitewashed sepulchres outa' here, they'll give the place a bad name.' And before the priests know what's hit them Lazarus, aided by Peter and Andrew, manhandle them towards the door. 'And while you're at it,' hollers M.M., 'there's a water trough outside, see if you can get rid of that smell – if the camels don't object, that is.'

And as the crowd follow to see the fun Jesus slips out of a side door unnoticed, leaving M.M. leaning over the balcony above the camel trough and Martha alone, on her knees, praying. Ruth is sleeping like a baby.

CHAPTER XII

Judas' Bag

nd what were Mike and Gaby doing while all this was going on? Well, they weren't resting on their laurels, that's for sure. In fact they were looking out for Satan. The jamming they had experienced earlier was definitely coming from somewhere within the brothel, so unless he had the power to make himself invisible, which was highly unlikely, he must have assumed a disguise. So who was the prime suspect? The Robots decided by a process of elimination and ended up with the odd man out – the Roman Centurion.

'But why would he draw attention to himself by choosing such a distinctive disguise?' asked Mike, reconsidering.

'Arrogance,' said Gaby, zooming into a close-up of him. They watched him intently for any give-away signs as he mounted his horse outside the brothel where Lazarus, Peter and Andrew were dunking the priests in the camel trough, much to the amusement of all the onlookers including the Centurion who laughed uproariously at the appeals of the priests for him to assert his authority and put Lazarus under arrest.

'My allegiance is to Rome and to Caesar, not to a bunch of Jewish hypocrites dressed to kill,' he retorted.

'But how about those guys?' Gaby exclaimed. 'How do we know those priests are kosher? Look at those beehive hats. Who knows what's hidden under them – could be anything from a high-tech jamming device to a pair of oxygen cylinders!'

'Nice theory,' said Mike a moment before the three priests lost their hats in the scuffle, 'but as you can see all they were hiding were three bald pates and anyway, sweetie, I hardly think Chief Priest Ezekiel is our man, do you?'

'Don't sweetie me,' snapped Gaby, 'and whoever Satan is he's a lot smarter than you . . . and me. I'm sorry, Mike,' she continued in contrite mode, 'I guess the strain of all this is beginning to get to me.' And for a moment she looked as if she might break down.

'That's all right, old girl, I understand,' said Mike, gently patting her on the shoulder – *boom, boom* – she sounded like an empty oil drum and you'd never guess she had a pacemaker and that it was beating faster since Mike had touched her.

'Better see what our boy is up to, I guess,' she said, switching off her emotive circuit and switching on the odourometer. Mike wisely kept silent and joined her in gazing at the monitor screen where the figure of Jesus was striding away from the village with Peter and Andrew running to catch up with him.

'What are your names?' asked Jesus.

'I am Peter,' said the more rugged of the men. 'And this is my brother Andrew.'

'We are fishermen,' added the latter.

'So you're not afraid of roughing it, getting wet, braving storms?'

'We can take care of ourselves, if that's what you mean,' said Peter.

'What do you want us to do, go back and give those priests a proper thrashing?' said Andrew eagerly. 'By the time we've finished with them even their own mothers won't know them!'

'They'll never dare show their noses around here ever again,' said Peter, shaking a fist as big as a ham-bone.

Jesus laughed, slowed to a stop and sat down on a boulder on the bank of a river and looked at them evenly. 'You know that old saying – "Love your friends, hate your enemies"?' They nodded expectantly. 'Well, I have news for you,' said Jesus. 'Whoever dreamed that up got it all wrong . . . ' The brothers looked puzzled. 'You should love your enemies and pray for those who screw you.' The brothers were shocked. 'God makes the sun rise on the good and bad alike and sends pissing rain down on the innocent as well as the guilty. So what's the big deal about only loving people who love you? Even the Romans do that. You must be perfect, just like your father in Heaven is perfect.' The brothers were stunned. 'Now, what can I do for you?'

The brothers looked at each other, hoping the other would speak first. Finally Peter took the plunge. 'I don't . . . What happened back there was . . . ' He became tongue-tied, so Andrew completed his thought.

'We couldn't just leave you like that. We . . . We wanted . . . '

' . . . Wanted to see what other tricks I had up my sleeve,' suggested Jesus ruefully. And as he waited for the brothers to sort out their thoughts and put them into words his attention turned towards a new arrival from the brothel. He was short and wiry, with a heavy sack thrown over one shoulder and a broad friendly smile creasing his face. 'Greetings, Master,' he said affably, dropping his sack to the ground. 'I have come to join you. What I saw back there was miraculous . . . '

' . . . and you'd like to go into business with me in a venture called "Miracle Wines", with me producing the product and you marketing it,' smiled Jesus.

'Such a thought never entered my head,' protested the newcomer as the brothers grinned. 'But it's not a bad idea all the same,' he continued roguishly. 'No, it was the way you dealt with those hypocrites, it did my heart a power of good. I'd like to know more about you.'

'Who are you?' asked Jesus.

'Oh, I've been many things in my time,' said the new-comer. 'Jack of all trades.'

'What have you got in that sack?' asked Jesus.

'All my worldly possessions,' replied the newcomer with a laugh.

'If you want to serve me and become one of my followers you must get rid of all your worldly possessions and . . .'

'No problem,' the newcomer cut in with a whoop as he snatched up the heavy sack and with a surprising show of strength whirled it around his head before casting it high in the air. Everyone watched as it plummeted into the river with a mighty splash and sank from sight. Impressed by his show of commitment, Peter found his tongue and a big question for Jesus.

'But what about our families? Are we expected to give them up too?'

'We'll be travelling light, living rough – we're going on a mission not a picnic,' said Jesus.

That was a tough one and the brothers mulled it over in their minds. Jesus turned to the newcomer. 'Does that bother you?'

'Not at all,' he replied. 'I'm as free as a bird.'

'What's your name?' asked Jesus.

'My name is Judas,' he replied with an open smile. 'How shall we address you?'

'Who do you say I am?' asked Jesus, turning to the brothers.

The brothers hesitated, looking at each other for support – almost afraid to put into words their innermost thoughts.

'You are the man prophesied by John the Baptist,' ventured Andrew.

'You are our blessed saviour,' ventured Peter, eyes shining, 'come to intercede between man and God.'

'And what's your guess?' asked Christ, turning to Judas who bowed his head in humility before replying.

'I would rather hear from your own lips the words I am unworthy to speak, Lord.'

Jesus sensed a trick question but came out with a straight answer nevertheless. 'I am Jesus Christ, son of God.'

At this Judas dropped to his knees, closely followed by Andrew and Peter.

Up above, our metal manipulators observe it all in close-up on their monitors.

'Are you thinking what I'm thinking?' murmured Gaby.

'I'm thinking Satan is standing right there in the flesh and he's just got rid of the evidence,' said Mike.

'The device he used to jam our laser beams, you mean?' said Gaby.

'Right, but then again, surely he wouldn't dump valuable equipment just like that,' reasoned Mike.

'Well, there's only one way to find out,' said Gaby. 'And that's to take a look for ourselves.'

'If you're thinking of teleporting that sack from the river bed there's the insulating effect of the water to overcome for a start, and then . . . '

'I know all that,' interrupted Gaby. 'I was thinking of e.m.f.'

'Yeah, that's fine if the stuff in the sack is made of metal, but if not . . . ' and Mike's shoulders rose and fell with a clunk, as much as to say, 'what then?'

'Well, it won't take long to give it a whirl, will it?' Gaby said, starting a programme.

'Just as soon as Jesus and the boys have gone,' said Mike, stating the obvious.

As it happened they didn't have long to wait before Jesus and his three followers hit the road in search of more disciples. Moments later the ship was hovering over the spot where Judas had thrown the sack. *Klunk* went a hunk of metal the size of a manhole cover as it was detached from the hull and lowered into the water on an electric cable. When it reached the river bed the magnet was energised and hauled up to reveal a truly bizarre sight. No, not the mystery contents of Judas' sack but the decomposing corpse of a Roman soldier in body armour with a knife sticking in his back. When they saw this on their monitor screen the Robots shuddered and killed the current – *sploosh* – returning the one-time guardian of the Roman Empire back to his watery grave.

'Obviously not very popular with the natives,' remarked Gaby.

'I guess no army of occupation ever is,' replied Mike. 'As for the contents of that sack, it looks like they'll have to remain a mystery.'

CHAPTER XIII

At the Pax Romana
Pizza Parlour

e'll have to monitor that Judas character real close,' said Gaby. 'I reckon he's got a hidden agenda.'

'Let's see what's he's up to now,' urged Mike. 'Get him on the odourometer.' And as quick as a sniff, there he was on a monitor screen in close-up and full stereo sound.

'Thanks a bunch. You can keep that Roman crap, wholesome Israeli nosh is good enough for me,' exclaimed Judas to someone off screen. 'I'll have the Rabbi Pie and a double order of Dead Sea Rolls.'

★

Gaby tapped into Mike's thought box and zoomed out for a wider picture. Mike buzzed his thanks.

It was lunch time at the Pax Romana, a little roadside pizza parlour where Jesus and the lads had just stopped off for a quick bite.

'Make mine an Amalfi Hot,' said Peter to the cute waitress.

'And I'll settle for the Nostra Mare Combo,' said Andrew.

'And I'd like a Lasagne à la Romana with a Caesar salad on the side,' said Jesus.

'Come on, guys,' said Judas when the waitress was out of earshot, 'you sound like a bunch of Roman tourists. This is like dining with the enemy.' There was a silence. Peter and Andrew waited for Jesus to speak up but he remained silent, waiting to see if the mini-sermon he preached to the brothers back at the river bank had sunk in . . . It had.

'Jesus says we should love our enemies,' said Peter.

'God makes the sun to shine on the good and bad alike,' added Andrew.

'What the fuck's that got to do with it?' exclaimed Judas. 'They come over here, defile our Temples with their pagan Gods, take all the best seats at the games, screw our women, cripple us with taxes and crucify our patriots. Look at Barabbas! He stood up and spoke his mind and now he's on death row waiting for the chop. And somehow we've got to save him . . . But *how*, that's the question. How!'

'Through prayer,' said Jesus simply.

'Prayer,' spat Judas as if it were a maggot in an apple. 'We've spent the last two thousand fucking years in prayer and we're still on our knees. For two millennia we've prayed you would come and here you are at last. Don't let us down, Master, it's time for action and time's running out.'

'I'm with you there,' said Jesus. 'The harvest is plentiful but the labourers few.'

'Does that mean you need more disciples, Master?' asked Peter.

'Yes, we need more voices to spread the word.'

'And the word is love, is it not, Master?' ventured Andrew.

'In all its guises,' beamed Jesus. 'What's up, Judas? You don't look happy. Do you Zealots have a problem with the "L" word?'

'No, Master,' he replied, 'but "L" also stands for liberty.'

'And . . .' said Jesus with an air of one about to proclaim a great revelation, '"L" also stands for . . . Lasagne à la Romana and here it comes with all the other goodies.' Everyone laughed as the tension was broken and the steaming food was laid on the table.

But up in the spaceship they were not laughing.

'I spy a fly in the ointment,' said Gaby.

' . . . And it's thrown a spanner in the works,' added Mike.

'That Judas has to be Satan,' said Gaby, 'set on undoing all our good work.'

'You could be right,' said Mike. 'Although it could just

be a coincidence, there are plenty of his kind around –
what did Jesus call him?'

'A Zealot,' said Gaby, flashing the meaning of the
word up on the screen. *Zealot, member of fanatical Jewish
sect dedicated to overthrowing their Roman overlords. Also
opposed to the Pharisees.*

'Pharisees, Schmarisees,' murmured Gaby, replacing
Zealot with Pharisee: *Member of Jewish religious sect dis-
tinguished by strict observance of traditional and written law,
pretensions to sanctity and self-righteousness.*

'Well, at least the two J's should see eye to eye on
those creeps,' said Gaby. 'Let's hope the rest of the disciples don't all turn out to be as stroppy as this one.'

'What's happening now?' asked Mike, prompting
Gaby to cut back to the pizza parlour where . . . Jesus
was just about to pick up the bill.

'Uh-huh,' exclaimed Gaby, activating the long-range
metal detector and focusing it on Jesus. 'Just as I thought,
not a penny in his pocket.'

'Teleport him a few shekels,' suggested Mike, 'or
we're going to have the Messiah washing up.'

But Gaby was way ahead of him.

By the time Jesus put his hand in his pocket it was jin-
gling with newly minted coins.

'Thank you, sir,' said the cute waitress, pocketing the
money, 'that's exactly right.' And she smiled sweetly but
showed no sign of moving.

The Robots were the first to get the reason why.

'She wants a tip and he has no change,' said Gaby.

'Better put a few more shekels in his pocket,' said Mike. 'And make it quick.'

'Hang on a minute,' said Gaby, curious to see the Messiah's next move.

But Jesus didn't get it and didn't move at all and neither did his disciples.

'Gratuities at your discretion, sir,' said the cute waitress, spelling it out with an even bigger smile. With a start Jesus finally woke up to what she wanted and dived his hand back into his pocket.

'Standby to teleport ten shekels,' ordered Mike.

'Aw, come on, Mike,' protested Gaby, 'this guy's blackmailing us. Let's make him sweat a little – throw him back on his own resources.'

'Do you really think we should?' wondered Mike. 'We can't let him lose face, especially not in front of his disciples.'

But as they ponder the waitress prospers.

'Thank you for your consideration,' said Jesus, shaking her hand.

'Thank you, sir,' replied the waitress, opening her hand to find it full of coins.

All are astonished, the Robots most of all, though Gaby plays it down.

'Mary Magdalene was right,' she scoffed. 'He's a magician. That was nothing but a cheap party trick – anyone can palm a few coins.'

'I agree,' said Mike, scratching his old tin head. 'It's where they came from that puzzles me.'

'Where are they off to now?' asked Gaby, evading the issue.

Down below, Judas was asking Jesus the same question.

'We're off to the Celestial City,' said Jesus, rising from the table.

'Is that another name for Paradise?' asked Peter.

'Yes,' said Jesus. 'We'll build a staircase.'

'We're gonna make it at any price,' enthused Andrew.

'With a good deed every day,' continued Jesus, leading the way up the hill.

'And we're on our fuckin' way,' roared Judas exuberantly.

'Nice sentiments,' said Mike as he watched them go.

'You could almost set them to music,' added Gaby.

CHAPTER XIV

The Stiff
Takes a Stroll

he next step Jesus took on his climb up those golden stairs was to find another disciple and so on and so on until he'd collected a round dozen. They came from all walks of life and death – for one was a taxman whose life was always under the threat of death because he worked for the Romans. So when Jesus said, 'Leave your job and follow me,' he wasn't slow in coming forward. His name was Matthew. Then there was Simon, a hot-headed Zealot a lot like Judas; then there were James and John who were fishermen like their friends Peter and Andrew; then there was Bartholomew, a baker who specialised in

hot-cross buns (later on in life); Thomas, who doubted
that he was ready to come out of the closet and Philip
who had come out years ago and didn't care who knew
it; then there was another James, the brother of John,
always getting confused with the other James; and
finally Thaddeus, who had a terrible stutter and was
mimicked mercilessly by everyone, especially when
they shouted Tha-Thad-Thaddeus – Judas being the
worst offender. They were a mixed bag recruited
mainly in pubs and wine bars where Jesus frequently
consorted with republicans and sinners. In other words,
politicians and tarts.

Then Jesus gave them a crash-course in faith-healing
and door-to-door evangelism, everything from acupunc-
ture to the parables. And it wasn't long before they were
proficient in the former and almost word perfect in the
latter. Imagine, if you will, a typical scene at an oasis
where Jesus is testing his pupils, who are almost ready to
graduate from the College of Christianity. Jesus sits on a
rock dangling his feet in the cooling waters of a pool as
his class of converts sits on the other side in the shade of
the sheltering palms.

Jesus speaks. '"And as the sower sowed his seed some
fell on stony ground and was snapped up by the birds" –
What is that like, children of Israel?'

Smiling, the disciples reply in unison: 'That is like the
person who hears the word of God but rejects the message.'

'Well done, lads,' says Jesus with a smile, 'let's continue. "And some seed fell among weeds which choked
its growth." What is that like?'

'That is like . . . ' the disciples chorus in unison, ' . . . a person who is choked by worldly goods, greed and gluttony.'

'Well done,' says Jesus. 'Now tell me about the seed that fell on the soil that was consumer-friendly.'

'That is like a person who listens to the word of God and grows in peace and love,' they reply to a man – even Thaddeus who has miraculously lost his stutter.

'Congratulations,' says Jesus, 'at last you are ready!'

'As ready as they'll ever be,' remarked Gaby, high in the sky above them.

'Shush,' retorted Mike, intent on the Messiah's every word.

' . . . Ready to go forth to heal the sick and sell the good news. But it won't be an easy task, believe me,' continues Jesus. 'You will be like sheep going to meet a pack of wolves, you'll be molested, mugged and maybe even murdered, all for my sake. But remember, they may destroy your body but they can never kill your soul. Sparrows are two a penny but not one of them falls to the ground without God's notice.' Jesus looks at their troubled faces and softens. 'Don't fret, you are worth a lot more than any sparrow. Now, are you still ready to join me?'

The disciples hesitate as the enormity of their crusade begins to sink in – deep.

'I think he's blown it,' said Mike.

'It's crunch time,' said Gaby.

*

Jesus repeated his question to the disciples who stared at him, petrified. 'Answer, are you still ready to join me?' Silence . . . broken . . . finally . . . by the voice of . . . a female: 'I am,' said Mary Magdalene, stepping from behind a palm tree . . . walking boldly up to Jesus and kissing him full on the mouth. More silence – pregnant.

'Take five,' said Jesus to his disciples, whereupon the silence instantly gives away to a buzzing like a swarm of bees as the disciples are blown away by the big smackeroo. Even the Robots get a buzz.

'Do I take it you really want to join up?' said Jesus with a wry smile.

'Sure thing,' said M.M., 'unless it's strictly a stag party you're into here.'

'You can't believe I'm sexist,' protested Jesus.

'You must be about the only man for a million miles who isn't,' she replied.

At that moment Judas sidled up to see if he was missing something. They both ignored him.

'What about your girls?' asked Jesus.

'Martha's taking care of them,' said M.M.

'And how's your big brother Lazarus?' Jesus asked politely.

'Lazarus is dead.'

Jesus was shocked. 'Why didn't you send word he was ill? I'd have come straight over.'

'He was bumped off,' came the curt reply.

Jesus was stunned. But not so Judas who had been taking it all in.

'I guess you can't throw a chief priest into a camel trough and expect to get away with it,' he declaimed.

'They must have sent one of their hit-men to rub him out in revenge.'

'Could be,' said M.M. coldly, 'he was stabbed in the back in a dark alley.'

'Bastards,' spat Judas, 'they're no better than the bloody Romans.'

'Where is the body?' asked Jesus, striking a more practical note.

'We buried him in the Valley of Eternal Rest,' said M.M., naming a popular graveyard a few miles back up the road.

'Why are you here, Mary?' asked Jesus. 'Do you expect me to conjure him back to life?'

'Not after four days, man,' she said. 'He was beginning to smell like a bad case of Camembert.'

'I am the resurrection and the life,' said Jesus. 'Those who believe in me shall live even though they die. Do you believe, Mary?'

It would have been easy for M.M. to answer 'yes', but scepticism dies hard so she hedged her bets, smiled and gave an honest answer.

'Well, you know what they say, Jesus, "Seein' is believin'."'

'And I say whoever lives and believes in me will never die.'

'Amen,' said the disciples, who had gathered around to listen.

As they all hurried away to the burial ground the Robots seemed to groan – or was it just the sound of stressed-out metal fatigue?

'We're dead,' said Mike.

'The scrap yard beckons,' said Gaby.

'R.I.P.,' said Mike.

'Rust in Peace,' added Gaby.

'We've met our Waterloo,' added Mike, piling on the agony.

'The trouble with "our boy",' said Gaby, with a touch of steel in her voice, 'is that he's beginning to suffer delusions of grandeur.'

'Doesn't he know that in the entire history of the universe nobody has ever reactivated dead matter?' said Mike.

'There's a first time for everything,' chirped Gaby, ever optimistic. 'Let's have a go.'

'What have we got to lose?' said Mike, switching on his 'brave' face. 'Let's go.'

By the time they got a fix on the desolate, boulder-strewn landscape known as the Valley of Eternal Rest it was swarming with sightseers and other interested parties. Word had got about that Jesus was going to raise the dead, and apart from those blessed with a morbid curiosity, the Jewish Mafia had also put in an appearance. This was the Mob that ran all the religious rackets in Jerusalem and most of the scams in the rest of the country. The fact that they were all dressed as priests fooled only a few. And the fact that the Godfather 'Chicken-Shit' Caiaphas was dressed as a high priest fooled no one at all. Caiaphas had parted with plenty of moolah to have Lazarus rubbed out and was on hand to demand a refund from his hit-men should the stiff take a stroll. He also wanted to keep an eye on Jesus who he had reason to fear. As for Ezekiel, the henchman who'd put the finger on Lazarus, well, he was conspicuous by his absence – in case anyone made the connection.

Such a person might have been the Centurion who had witnessed the incident at the camel trough and was on hand with a detachment of Roman troops itching to kick ass in case of trouble.

A buzz of speculation swarmed through the crowd as M.M. led Jesus up to the entrance of a cave, one of many carved into the hillside, which contained the mummified corpse of her dear departed brother. Quickly, Judas organised the more butch of the disciples to roll away the boulder sealing the entrance. And judging by their creased faces the body was maturing nicely. It was then the seriousness of the situation manifested itself and the carnival atmosphere disappeared on an ill wind.

Meanwhile Mike and Gaby were busy racking their racing Robotic brains.

'Do we have Lazarus' brain-print?' queried Mike.

'Negative,' said Gaby, 'but I know what you're thinking and it wouldn't work. We'll have to take a chance and link him to central singularity.'

Mike shook his head. 'The risk is too great. If we damage the body Christ's reputation would be gone for good.'

'I'll scan the cave,' said Gaby, not to be put off. 'Maybe there's some other dead matter we can experiment on.

Yes, look over there – that rat rotting in the corner, see it?'

'I see it,' said Mike, reluctantly activating the target monitor and getting the rodent in his sights.

'Permission to activate central singularity?' snapped Gaby.

'Affirmative,' said Mike, aware that he was dicing with death.

Instantly, Gaby programmed the first half of the combination on a wall-safe, coloured red for danger, then rapidly changed places with Mike who only knew the second half of the combination, which he punched in pronto. Throwing open the door he revealed a single red switch which he immediately grabbed hold of before turning to Gaby who had the rat in her sights.

'Ready?' he demanded.

'Fire!' she shouted.

Mike took a deep breath and threw the switch. Glass eyes full of hope they gazed at the rat on the monitor screen only to see it melt into something that looked like steaming diarrhoea.

Sadly, Mike switched off the current and closed the heavy metal door. *Clunk!*

'Thank the Lord we didn't try it out on Lazarus,' muttered Mike, trying to rescue a crumb of consolation from the abortive effort.

'Yep, Jesus would have been in deep shit,' said Gaby, breaking into a giggle.

And as he watched the running rat-crap Mike found it hard not to giggle too. And in next to no time they were rattling around the place giggling fit to burst a gut.

'Lazarus, come out,' Jesus boomed suddenly in surround sound, instantly sobering them up.

'Wake me when it's over,' said Mike. 'I can't look, I'm shutting down.'

'Don't be chicken,' shouted Gaby, 'he'll think of something – say it's "God swill" or something.' Too late. Mike was completely out of it, just part of the furniture. Gaby steeled herself to face the monitor showing the mouth of the cave and the black, silent emptiness beyond. Silence, too, from the crowd as time almost stood still. Then came a thunderous fart that seemed to rock around the universe as Lazarus, still unseen, expelled all the highly toxic gas in his body as he lurched off the slab that was to have been his last resting place. Covered in winding bandages from head to foot, all seven foot of him, he staggered jerkily to the mouth of the cave and sunlight.

'The mummy lives,' shouted Gaby joyously, reactivating Mike. 'The mummy lives!'

'What, what? I've seen it,' said Mike, convinced he was looking at the old Boris Karloff movie of the same name!

'This is no movie, this is real,' shouted Gaby, excitedly pointing at the monitor where Lazarus had now come to a bewildered stop.

'Cast off the bonds of death,' commands Jesus theatrically. 'He lives.'

Suddenly the mob go mad. And while Peter and Andrew tear off the bandages M.M. kisses her brother's feet, hands and face, as the crowd roar their approval.

★

Equally euphoric are the Robots.

'It's a miracle,' said Mike.

'Did you hear what you said?' laughed Gaby.

'What, what did I say?' asked Mike.

'You said, you said,' said Gaby, barely able to contain herself, 'you said "IT'S A MIRACLE".'

'I said "it's a miracle"?' repeated Mike, finally getting the joke. 'We're the ones that work miracles and we . . . we . . . ' And they both began to sober up at the implication.

' . . . We blew it,' said Gaby.

'Then who . . . ?' said Mike, leaving Gaby to answer the question for him.

'Satan, of course – and just take a look at Judas, will you. If he was any closer to Jesus he'd be in back of him.'

This was not strictly true, but as the prime suspect he was pretty well placed to practise some Dr Frankenstein-type therapy. But Mike, never one to jump to conclusions, zoomed out for a wider perspective, revealing suspect number two. Yes, as we know already, the horseman in charge of the detachment of Roman troops is our friendly Centurion – poised to take care of the trouble brewing.

The cause of the disturbance is due to the Godfather – the lone voice of High Priest Caiaphas – heaping venom and abomination, hellfire and damnation on the spotlit (due to the sun pouring through a small gap in the clouds) figure of Jesus, who is standing in shining white on a mound of rock outside the burial chamber.

'This man has defiled the sabbath,' screams Caiaphas, who is completely freaked. 'The sabbath is a day of rest devoted to the praise of God and in working to raise the dead you have broken his holy law.' This is an extremely serious allegation, as everyone present knows, and there is silence as the crowd breathlessly awaits Christ's reply.

'If a sheep falls into a ditch on the sabbath, does the shepherd leave it there to die?' demands Jesus. His audience scoffs at the very idea. Jesus continues, 'I am the shepherd sent into the world by my father to tend *his* flock – even on the sabbath.' The silence is now thunderous, this is the ultimate blasphemy punishable by death. The storm breaks – Caiaphas and the Mob scream and howl like the hounds of hell while those who have seen the evidence of their own eyes and believe in the Lord shout Jesus' praises and flock towards him, elbowing Caiaphas and his cronies out of the way as they go. Moments later the Centurion has a full-scale riot on his hands.

'That's put the cat among the pigeons,' observed Mike gloomily.

'Not to worry,' replied Gaby. 'A bird in the hand is worth two in the bush.' Mike nodded in agreement although he hadn't a clue what she meant; Gaby's metaphor programming left much to be desired. 'Shall we intervene?' suggested Gaby, getting practical again. 'I'd love to kick the shit out of Caiaphas and his crew.'

'We're on a peace mission, remember,' admonished Mike gently.

'Anything for a little light relief, sir,' said Gaby with a bright little smile. 'There are times when all this starts to get to me.' Mike looked at her, was about to speak, then thought better of it. But Gaby read his thoughts.

'If you say I'm suffering from P.M.T.* I'll brain you,' she said, 'so help me.'

'No, not at all, I won't, I wasn't,' stammered Mike. 'I was just going to say . . . er, the Romans seem to have got things under control – situation normal.'

Still simmering, Gaby let it pass and settled down to watch the continuing events on the monitor, which were turning out to be as entertaining as any soap she had ever seen on Rossum's Galaxy TV.

Like rival fans at a football match the supporters have been segregated by the law and sent back home – all save M.M., Lazarus and the disciples who have been confined to the cave and Jesus who has been brought before the Centurion for a private one-to-one. Surprisingly he invites Jesus to take a seat on a rock beside him.

---

* Pre-Mesolithic tension

CHAPTER XV

Women!

'o, we meet again,' said the Centurion, treating Jesus to a frosty smile. 'From a hand-job to necrophilia in less than a fortnight. I'm impressed.'

'The metaphor of a military man,' remarked Jesus with a smile, 'but I get your drift.'

Glad that Jesus took his crude jest in good heart, the Centurion came straight to the point.

'I have a slave, a good worker, honest, faithful, sick as a dog and impossible to replace. I need your help.'

'Is this slave close at hand?' asked Jesus.

'Jerusalem,' said the Centurion.

'Two days' journey,' said Jesus, sounding a note of despondency.

'So what?' said the Centurion.

'We may be too late,' said Jesus.

'Let me spell it out for you,' said the Centurion, verging on impatience. 'You and I have much in common, we both command respect, we both speak with authority, I say to a man "go" and he goes, "come" and he jerks off. I give an order in Jerusalem for a man to be crucified in Caesarea and he's crucified in Caesarea. Surely you can do the same to save my slave? Just call long-distance.'

Jesus smiled and chanced his arm. 'Why not save yourself, Centurion, by joining my dream-team? Your faith in my powers would help win many converts and bring them salvation.'

'What, leave the Roman Army to join the Salvation Army! I'd be executed as a deserter! Besides, I doubt if the pay's as good.'

'There's no pay at all,' replied Jesus, 'but I can promise you a good time in Paradise.'

'Pie in the sky,' said the Centurion with a laugh. 'Are you going to do it or not?'

And as Jesus paused to consider his reply, Mike and Gaby paused to consider their problem.

'Well, at least we've got time on our side to try and sort something out,' said Mike.

'Look's like the old odourometer's going to be working overtime,' said Gaby, who was already busy analysing the myriad scents emanating from both the Centurion's body and his uniform – everything from cunt to cockroaches. A moment later the Robots were hovering over the Barracks Romana in Jerusalem where, they reasoned, the Centurion must be posted.

Sure enough the odourometer registered a strong signal, and as the scanner honed into Max Stink a bell rang. Simultaneously a picture of the exact location popped up on the monitor revealing the Centurion's quarters, comprising three rooms and a stand-up loo. The fact that a female was lying in bed came as no great surprise to the Robots, neither did the fact that she was covered in bumps and bruises. A quick X-ray also revealed internal bruising but nothing so serious that our space-vets couldn't cure it with a little instant therapy – which had the slave back on her knees scrubbing floors before Jesus could say to the Centurion—

'Go in peace and give my blessing to your slave, and in future treat her with the same respect with which you would treat your own sister – we're all brothers and sisters under the skin.'

Stunned, the Centurion is momentarily speechless – Jesus' cool gaze seems to pin his very soul to the back of his skull. But the moment passes and the Centurion once more regains his cool.

'You and your disciples are free to go,' he says. 'But if I have any more trouble from you I'll crucify you with my own hands, understood?'

'Understood,' says Jesus calmly.

Up above, Mike and Gaby were also stunned. 'How did he know the slave was a woman?' wondered Mike aloud.

'God knows,' replied Gaby. 'Guessed it, I guess, or maybe he can read our minds.'

'We don't have minds, remember,' said Mike.

'Sorry, for a moment I forgot,' said Gaby.

For a while they were silent, busy spinning fantastic patterns in their memory banks, which was as close as they ever came to daydreaming. And those patterns always evolved into Satan.

Satan was an enigma. They weren't even certain who he was. Sometimes they thought he was Judas, sometimes the Centurion, and now Gaby had a theory it might be M.M. After all, she'd been around for all the major events in which Satan had a hand.

'Tell you what,' whispered Mike. 'Maybe it's none of them. Maybe . . . ' and he lowered his voice even lower ' . . . maybe it's in this very ship.'

'You mean it's a bug, a bug that has infiltrated the entire system. That would mean we're at the mercy of a schizophrenic computer,' whispered Gaby.

'Well, we've all heard about the "Deus ex machina",' said Mike. 'Maybe there's a "Diabolus ex machina".'

'Sorry, you've lost me,' said Gaby, who had not been programmed in Latin, 'but if you mean we're being manipulated, then say so. Personally I think we're doing just fine despite all the interference. Maybe it's nothing worse than an interplanetary poltergeist out for a bit of fun. You know how playful they can be.'

Mike let that one pass. In his youth he'd been a ghost-buster and had come up against many psychic phenomena, but not one of them had the power to resurrect the dead. So who could it be? Then he thought the impossible and dismissed it from his mind. Night was falling – time to quit idle speculation and press on.

'What say we run a health-check on Lazarus?' he suggested to Gaby.

'Roger,' she replied and went into action on the odourometer.

'My Lord, he's back in the tomb,' she exclaimed.

'Let's pray he hasn't had a relapse,' muttered Mike.

'If he has, then he's got a hulluva lot of mourners keeping him company,' said Gaby as she zoomed past a barbecue at the cave mouth to the candle-lit interior . . . where the convalescent corpse was all washed and dressed and happily chewing on a haunch of roasted billy goat, surrounded by the disciples partying away like there was no tomorrow.

'I wonder where the food and drink came from?' said Mike.

'God knows,' said Gaby. 'Can you see the Messiah?' She continued scanning the joyful faces. 'I can't, can you?'

'No, and I can't see M.M. either,' said Mike. 'Maybe they've gone for a breath of fresh air.'

'More like a bit of nooky,' said Gaby. 'Do you want I should check 'em out on the odourometer?'

'Guess we'd better,' said Mike. 'After that run in with the Godfather chances are he's top of their hitlist.'

'I'm more worried about M.M. than the Mafia,' said Gaby, getting agitated. 'Shit, I can't pick him up, her neither – the odourometer's malfunctioning.'

And with the Robots temporarily blinded by science, as it were, it is time for us to take a look for ourselves. It was as they supposed: Jesus and M.M. were strolling arm in arm under the stars.

'How can I ever repay you?' asked M.M. softly.

That was a serious question so Jesus gave it serious thought, but M.M. took his silence for shyness so made a proposal of her own.

'It's a nice night for a freebie, should you feel so inclined, Jesu.'

Jesus gave her a kindly smile that made her day. 'Ours will have to be a spiritual union, Mary, I've taken a vow of celibacy and if you think about it I'm sure you'll figure out why.'

They walked on in silence for a while as M.M. pondered some.

'Well,' she said finally, 'something tells me that it's not in your nature to practise safe sex, so I guess that could have embarrassing consequences. What if you sired a family with lots of Godsons popping up all over the place and working miracles and such – it would be mayhem . . . and dangerous as well, come to think of it. And if you fathered any Godettes it could be downright controversial. And I'm confused enough as it is; here am I, me, a tarnished tart tryin' to get it off with the son of God. May God forgive me if it's true.'

'How can he not forgive you, Mary?' said Jesus gently. 'I'm not the first man claiming to be sent from God and I won't be the last. You probably think I'm a nutcase.'

'The jury's still out on that one,' said M.M., 'but one thing's for sure, Lazarus is alive and kickin' and he'll sure kick some ass if ever he catches up with those Mobsters, and it's all thanks to you.'

'In all honesty I can't take *all* the credit,' said Jesus with a touch of irony.

'Well, next time you get in touch with your father ask him when he's going to get those Romans off our backs.'

'I'll certainly pass on the message,' said Jesus, smiling in the dark.

'And if he's lucky enough to have one, please give my regards to his wife,' she said, smiling right back.

And as they both rejoined the party the odourometer reactivated itself, just like that.

'Well, there's a coincidence,' said Mike.

'Or is it?' said Gaby.

And that's all she said, but Mike knew exactly what she was thinking about. It was the dreaded 'S' word.

CHAPTER XVI

Lox 'n' Bagels
for
Five Thousand

he next day was a big day, and no one was prepared for it – not even Satan.

At sun-up the first arrivals were already on the scene. Word of the miracle of Lazarus had got round. It was front-page news and all the sick that could limp, creep, crawl or cadge a lift within a fifty-mile radius of the Valley of Eternal Rest were on their way.

The morning was taken up with miracle cures and in this Jesus was joined by his disciples and, of course, the Robots, who worked overtime. And it could probably be said that the only one who didn't need outside help was M.M., who used her vast experience as an agony aunt and brothel keeper to act as marriage guidance counsellor and sex therapist. By noontime everyone, but everyone, was in danger of serious overheating, including them up there.

'Let's take a break, Lord,' suggested Peter. 'I'm beat.'

'D'you want I break it up, Jesus?' asked Judas. 'I could kill for a goat burger.'

'But what about the people?' said the ever-thoughtful Messiah. 'They've been up for hours, we can't send them all away on empty stomachs. Haven't we got some leftovers from last night's party?'

Everyone hunted high and low but all they came up with was some lox and bagels at the bottom of a basket.

'That won't go far between five thousand, Lord,' said Peter sadly.

'None who come to my table shall go away hungry,' said Jesus, taking the basket, raising it to Heaven and muttering a silent prayer.

And Heaven, in the form of a hovering spacecraft, heard him. And the two willing angels within quickly set about doing his bidding.

'Shall we teleport an order of lox and bagels from a nearby town?' suggested Gaby.

'Good idea,' said Mike, 'but that would be stealing.'

Surprised at Mike's high moral tone, Gaby rolled her eyes but made no verbal comment.

'Then how's about we send down some form of substitute, like soya – they'll never know the difference.'

'Not after a little reorganisation,' smiled Mike, activating a video synthesiser.

Meanwhile the disciples were all agog as they prayed for a miracle while Jesus continued to hold the near-empty basket above his head. His arms began to ache as the Robots worked overtime with Mike moulding acceptable replicas of the raw material and Gaby going to town on the colour tinting.

'Right,' said Mike, 'programme the soya manipulator duplication system.'

'Roger,' said Gaby, getting to work.

'Programme copies for despatch at two-second intervals,' said Mike.

'Hang on,' said Gaby, 'I'm going flat out.'

By now Jesus was beginning to sweat, and so were the disciples. Mike was also beginning to feel the strain and wondered if they'd bitten off more than they could chew.

'Got it,' said Gaby, finally pushing *play*. 'Soya teleport operational.'

A split second later Jesus felt the basket a shade heavier as the first order arrived. With a sigh of relief he lowered the basket and stepped back.

'There, eat your fill, then feed the people.' And how the disciples marvelled as they helped themselves to the soya from Heaven that continued to arrive at two-second intervals. And apart from Judas lamenting the lack of sour cream they all loved it and because of a lifetime of conditioning their taste buds supplied the flavour their eyes led them to anticipate – despite the fact they were eating the same basic commodity.

★

'Well, that should keep them happy for a while,' observed Gaby. 'What next?'

'Time for the "message from our sponsor",' said Mike.

Evidently the crowd thought so too for, having filled their bellies and slaked their thirst in a convenient stream, they were now all chanting in unison: 'Jesus, Jesus, Jesus . . .'And Jesus, having climbed to the top of a hillock, visible to all, was ready to oblige. He held up his hand for silence and silence was what he got – even the birds in the air stopped their twittering.

'You are happy now because your bellies are full, but you can't live to the full on bread alone. Only by nour-ishing the spirit will you enjoy complete happiness. And that happiness will last for ever.'

'How shall we find this happiness?' asked a man close to Jesus. 'How shall we recognise it?'

'A brother over here wants to know what true happi-ness is,' said Jesus, raising his voice for all to hear. 'I will tell you what it means to be truly happy:

> *Happy are those who feel a need of God,*
> *for the Kingdom of Heaven is theirs.*
> *Happy are those who have known sorrow,*
> *for they will be given strength and comfort.*
> *Happy are those who are not greedy,*
> *for the whole world will be theirs.*
> *Happy are those who hunger for truth,*
> *for they shall be satisfied.*
> *Happy are those who show mercy to others,*
> *for they shall receive mercy from God.*

Happy are those who suffer persecution in the cause of
    truth,
for great will be their reward in Heaven.

'That is the meaning of happiness, brothers and sisters.
Rejoice and be glad.'

'Word-perfect,' gasped Gabby, brimming over with joy.
Mike said nothing; he couldn't – he was choked. All the
years of brainwashing through the microchip in Christ's
brain had not been in vain if the reaction of the crowd
was anything to go by; they were ecstatic.

Someone shouted, 'Christ the King!' And in a moment
everyone had taken up the cry, chanting, 'Christ the
King! Christ the King!' in a paean of praise. Even the
disciples were carried away as Jesus descended the
hillock to join them.

'The multitude has proclaimed you King, O Lord,'
enthused Peter. 'Let's march to Jerusalem.'

'This very night we shall see you enthroned in splendour,' gushed Andrew.

'We'll rub out Caiaphas and the Mob for ever,'
shouted Judas. Yells of encouragement and acclamation
followed as all the other disciples except M.M. joined in.
She alone remained subdued. Maybe she was mindful of
the danger from the Romans and the Mob, conspicuous
by their absence (they were bound to have spies and
informers around anyhow), or maybe she was just plain
psychic. Jesus also remained cool.

'I will not be crowned King by force,' he exclaimed.

'When the hour comes for me to enter Jerusalem it must be as foretold in the scriptures, and before that time we have much work to do. But first we have to dodge the crowds and the only way we can do that is by water. Peter, Andrew, you've got a boat; is it big enough to ferry us all across the Sea of Galilee?'

'Just about, Lord, but it'll be a tight squeeze,' said Peter, glancing pointedly at M.M. and Lazarus.

'Don't worry, they won't be coming along,' said Jesus. 'I have other plans for them.' Initially crestfallen, brother and sister perked up again.

'So,' continued Jesus, 'Philip to Canaan, Bartholomew to Tiberius, Thaddeus to Beersheba, James to Jericho, Judas to Capernaum, John to Judea, James, brother of John, to Hebron, Matthew to Bethsaida, Andrew to Gaza, Peter to Bethanay, Simon to Samaria and Thomas to Tyre. Spread the word, do good deeds and before you know it the Holy City will be ours.'

'Can't you be a bit more precise, Lord,' urged Judas, who was not at all happy with his posting.

'God will give us a sign,' said Jesus. 'Look towards Heaven. Have faith! We must be like stars shining in the darkness to light the way for those who are lost. Right! Time to move: Peter, lead the way to the boat. Andrew and I will join you later.'

All the disciples hesitated for a moment, it was all so sudden.

'Move it,' said Jesus abruptly, spurring them into action. 'I'll give you cover. Mary, Lazarus, follow me.' And while the disciples hurried away Jesus briefed

M.M. and Lazarus as they followed him up the hillock. On reaching the summit Jesus raised his hands for silence.

'I must leave you for a while,' said Jesus to the five thousand. 'The time has come for me to spread God's word throughout the land of Israel. Even so we can still be united through the love of our father in Heaven. Now give me your attention and repeat after me: Our father in Heaven.'

Mumbled confusion came as a response.

'Now get with it,' said Jesus. 'Concentrate!

'Our Father in Heaven . . .'

And with M.M. and Lazarus either side of Jesus leading the responses the rendering was much improved.

'Better,' said Jesus. 'Hallowed be your name.'

Even more improvement as the crowd caught on.

'Your Kingdom come.'

'Your Kingdom come,' thundered the massive response.

'That's it, go for it,' laughed Jesus. 'Your will be done on Earth as it is in Heaven.'

The response to that rattled the very bones of the dead in their tombs, and so it continued for the remainder of the prayer.

> 'Give us this day our daily bread,
> And forgive us our trespasses
> As we forgive them that trespass against us.
> Lead us not into temptation,
> But deliver us from evil.
> For yours is the Kingdom,

The Power and the Glory,
For ever and ever,
Amen.'

'Well done,' said Jesus. 'And next time say it as if you mean it. And to help you fix it in your minds, my good friends here will run you through it a few times. So until we meet again, just remember – all you need is love!'

Acclamation and jubilation rendered his farewells to M.M. and Lazarus inaudible but the joyful expressions on their faces told it all. And the happy noise continued as Jesus hurried off down the hillock to follow Andrew to the coast.

CHAPTER XVII

Running
on Water

ike and Gaby were over the moon –
literally. Knowing they had an hour
to themselves before Andrew and
Jesus arrived at the boat, they
decided to celebrate Christ's tri-
umphant session at the Valley of
Eternal Rest by treating themselves
to a tour of the local sights including the rings of Saturn
and the man in the moon – last survivor of one of
Rossum's less successful experimental species, now
doomed to extinction. How time flies when you are
enjoying yourself. By the time the Robots came down to

Earth Christ and the disciples were all at sea . . . in the heart of a storm.

'If they ship much more water they'll sink. You can't leave them alone for five minutes,' said Gaby, watching the pathetic efforts of the disciples to bail out with cupped hands. Christ alone was calm as, with eyes raised in the direction of the Robots, he prayed for dear life.

'We've got to act fast,' said Mike, beginning to panic. 'If the boat goes down we're sunk. Somehow we've got to calm the storm.'

'That means creating an anticyclone,' said Gaby, 'or, better still, a ridge of high pressure.'

'And just how do we do that?' asked Mike, hitting his 'don't panic' button.

'First I'll equalise the atmospheric pressure, then I'll use the Maser Rotator* to excite the molecules in the atmosphere,' said Gaby brightly as she started activating the programme.

'Good thinking,' said Mike. 'Meanwhile I'll work on a miracle cure for seasickness.'

'No need,' retorted Gaby. 'We should have settled weather conditions by 51.29 degrees.' And sure enough, in a little over two minutes (Earth time) the storm had abated and the sea had started to calm.

'Well,' said Gaby, killing the Maser Rotator, 'we've had the feeding of the five thousand, the raising of the

---

*The Maser Rotator is a device that gives off high-energy microwaves, transmitted in a lighthouse-beam fashion, stimulating the various energy levels of the molecules in the air.

dead, the calming of the storm. What next – walking on water?'

'Don't put ideas into his head,' said Mike.

Too late. Jesus was already toying with the idea. During the storm the oars had washed overboard and drifted astern. And clearly none of the disciples, all various shades of green, were fit to dive in and retrieve them. So as usual it was all down to Jesus, who was already preparing to step over the side. And in seconds the Robots were ready for him. It was simply a question of accurately tracking his movements with an anti-gravitational force sufficient to cancel out the strength of the Earth's gravitational pull, plus a little extra to put some bounce into his step when he strode across the water.

Anyone who has seen pictures of spacemen bouncing over the surface of the moon will readily get the picture. And Jesus bounced like a kid at the seaside. First he splashed around the boat to perk up the disciples, who were soon grinning with pleasure, and by the time he had skipped off to retrieve the oars they had cheered up no end.

'Can I join you, Master?' chortled Peter, itching to share in the fun.

'Be my guest,' said Jesus. 'All you need is faith.'

'Faith I have in buckets, Master,' said Peter, standing up.

'Quick, prepare to track him, too,' said Mike to Gaby.

'Check,' said Gaby.

★

Peter jumped out of the boat and stood on the water, to cheers from the others.

Suddenly they were all filled with the holiday spirit. The sun was shining, the water was calm and there wasn't a cloud in the sky. They all wanted a go.

'Standby to track the lot of them,' panicked Mike as they all prepared to take to the waters.

'Fuck that for a lark,' shouted Gaby. 'Soon they'll *all* be wanting to work miracles and we've got enough on our plates as it is just handling the Messiah.'

So the disciples sank like proverbial stones, spluttering and shouting as they all went under. Peter laughed till tears ran down his cheeks. 'Oh, you of little faith,' he roared.

'Peter's getting a bit too big for his boots,' murmured Mike.

'Shall I teach him a lesson?' said Gaby with a wicked smile.

'With pleasure,' said Mike.

'Here goes, then,' giggled Gaby – cutting the AGF current.

'Help, Lord,' shouted Peter, sinking fast. 'Help!'

But Jesus merely laughed as he made his way swiftly across the waters to step safely over the gunwale and into the boat. Then, setting down the oars, he turned to his floundering followers, who were screaming for help.

★

'I wonder how he'll get out of this one,' said Mike.

'With ease,' said Gaby. 'Just watch.'

'Why, Lord, why?' spluttered Peter, joining in the general chorus of disillusion.

'Why?' said Jesus, repeating the question with a smile. 'Because your faith was piss-poor, that's why.'

'I told you so,' said Gaby to Mike with a smile.

Jesus helped them back into the boat. Chastened, the damp disciples had plenty of food for thought as they sailed to the far shore of the Sea of Galilee. Soon they would be splitting up and setting off into the unknown.

The Robots were also concerned with their future.

'Looks like we'll have to divide ourselves into thirteen,' said Mike.

'An unlucky number according to poor superstitious humans,' said Gaby.

'The tide is turning, the word is spreading, the people are starting to follow,' said Mike. 'Even Satan seems to be backing off.'

'I wonder why?' said Gaby.

'Maybe he's getting bored with playing the bad guy,' said Mike. 'Maybe he's found fatter fish to fry.'

'Or maybe he just thinks we're not gonna make it,' said Gaby. 'Maybe he thinks the rot has set in too deep for us to do a salvage job.'

'He could be biding his time,' said Mike. 'Just waiting for the right moment to deliver that double-whammy.'

'I'm sure you're wrong,' said Gaby. 'Technologically he must be light years ahead of us.'

'Then why doesn't he just blow us away?' said Mike.

'I dunno,' said Gaby. 'Maybe he needs us in some strange way.'

'Whatever his reason we mustn't get complacent,' said Mike. 'Did you think to trace the power source that raised Lazarus?'

Gaby looked abashed and shook her sweet tin head. 'Sorry, I guess I was just too freaked.'

'That's OK, I should have thought of it myself,' said Mike, shouldering the blame. 'We gotta be more on the ball, that's all, or we'll never have peace on Earth and goodwill to all men.'

'Amen to that,' said Gaby, inadvertently slipping into Bible-speak like her captain.

CHAPTER XVIII

Palm Power

nd so the disciples spread the word and did good works with help from above and were both surprised and elated with their success. Meanwhile Jesus spent some quality time with his dad on the Mount of Olives. But it wasn't all plain sailing for the disciples who had a lot of aggro to put up with and more than once the Robots had to put the (invisible) boot in . . . Purely in the name of peace . . . Until one day . . . Gaby said, 'Apart from falling hair and dandruff we've cured every ailment in the book. I'm beginning to feel like Mother Theresa.'

'And I think Jesus is just about to OD on olives,' Mike observed. 'Shall we call it a day?'

'Great, let's go for the big picture,' enthused Gaby.

'Great,' echoed Mike.

'But first we need our audience,' said Gaby, 'so I'd like your OK to transmit an Alpha-burst homing signal to the individual brain frequency of each disciple that'll lead 'em straight back to the boss.'

'Who has conveniently dropped to his knees to call them in with a little telepathic prayer, bless his heart,' continued Mike patronisingly.

And sure enough, one by one, the disciples turned towards the Mount of Olives, and in the company of all their converts started hiking towards it.

By the time they had arrived a few days later the Robots were preparing to wow them with their high-tech white light hologram of the Celestial City.

'What's bothering you, Mike?' asked Gaby, noticing his furrowed brow.

'I'm a little concerned about image intensity – with all this sunshine around I'm afraid it's not going to register,' he said.

'No problem,' said Gaby. 'I'll start moving in a trough of low pressure.'

And as Jesus kneels in prayer and his followers fairly fly up the slope like a flock of homing pigeons the storm clouds gather, the sky darkens and the distant rumble of thunder is heard. Louder and louder it grows as it rolls ever closer – culminating in an enormous peal of sound as from a mighty organ. In fact it *is* the sound of a mighty organ improvised by Mike on his Rossumuki synthesiser high in the clouds above. And as he tops this awe-inspiring sound with a cymbal crash that all but shatters their ear drums Gaby blasts the sky apart with a million-watt flash from which the vision of the Celestial City grows in size and splendour with each succeeding second until it stretches from horizon to horizon and almost reaches Heaven itself. And as the thousands of instant converts watch goggle-eyed they are gently baptised in a soft refreshing rain that washes away their cares and elevates their spirits. A rainbow forms, seeming to spring from the kneeling figure of Jesus and arcs towards the City in the sky which glows ever brighter until it dissolves into the shining orb of an enormous sun which warms their hearts and dries their bodies.

It was a triumph, a spectacular triumph. For technical wizardry nothing was to equal it for the next two thousand years – until Hollywood made a movie called *Titanic*. However, that had nowhere the same uplift. And uplift was the order of the day. Everyone was on an enormous high – Robots and humans alike, because the moment had finally arrived for the Messiah and his followers to make that triumphal entry into Jerusalem.

'The time has come for us to march to the Holy City and establish our Kingdom on Earth,' said Jesus to the multitude. 'So grab yourselves a bunch of palm fronds so that folks can see we come as liberators who have no need of lethal weapons.'

And as the followers set off with whoops and yells of joy to do his bidding, Peter sounded a note of caution.

'But surely we need a few weapons for our own protection, Master?'

'What chance would thirteen armed men have against the fire-power of Herod and the Roman army?' replied Jesus. 'We are soldiers of Peace and will conquer with Love.'

Peter, ashamed of his momentary lack of faith, nodded silently, then made off to organise a working party.

Jesus turned to Andrew and pointed to some buildings at the foot of the hill. 'Get down to that farmhouse. In the yard you'll find a donkey. Bring it to me.'

'But they will take me for a thief, Master,' said Andrew.

'Say you need it for the Lord Jesus,' he replied. And Andrew bowed and went to do his bidding.

'I wish he'd chosen a more dignified mode of transport,' said Gaby as, a short time later, Jesus mounted the donkey. 'He looks kinda silly with his feet trailing the ground, don't you think?'

'I dunno,' said Mike, 'I think he looks kinda cute. Anyway, the prophet says "A King will come in peace riding on a donkey", and the prophecy must be fulfilled. How would *you* have him enter the Holy City?'

'I'd have him sail through the gates on a magic carpet,' said Gaby.

'You got your source material mixed up,' grinned Mike. 'This is the Old Testament we're dealing with here, *not* the Arabian Nights.'

They both smiled and turned their attention back to

the master monitor where a spectacle worthy of Cecil B. de Mille was unfolding on the screen before them – only the thousands of chanting supporters following the Messiah looked like real people, not extras, the sort you used to see with flowers in their hair at rock festivals in the 60s.

They praised him on the flutes, they praised him on the harp, they praised him on the cymbals and they praised him upon the loud cymbals. And such was the happy racket that it aroused the inhabitants of the city and brought them surging out of the Lion Gate to form an improvised welcoming committee. And as the fans of Jesus approached the city singing his praises, the song was taken up by those pouring out of the city.

'Blessed is he that comes in the name of the Lord. All glory to the true Messiah. Jesus . . . Jesus . . . Jesus . . . etc.'

Mike and Gaby fairly glowed with pride but, ever vigilant and blessed with the vision of hawks, they quickly detected a small group of spectators who watched the approaching army with something less than enthusiasm. They were dressed as priests and stood upon the ramparts of the Lion Gate that Jesus and his followers were about to pass under. They were actually members of the Mob – fronted by the Godfather, Caiaphas – who was deep in conversation with our glamorous Centurion, whom I forgot to mention could have passed for Charlton Heston's twin brother. Somewhat taken aback, the Robots zoomed in for a closer look-see at Caiaphas sounding off.

'Look at them, they're going bananas. You've got to do something about it and fast, they're a threat to law and order. Arrest them!'

'What for, waving palm leaves in the air?' laughed the Centurion. 'Get real.'

'The man's a fanatic, a nutter!' said Caiaphas heatedly, as Jesus passed from sight beneath them. 'He even claims to be King of the Jews.'

'Well, maybe he should be. Isn't he supposed to be descended from King David?' replied the Centurion. 'The only reason Herod's on the throne is because we put him there. We made him and we can break him. The people hate him anyway; all he can do is raise taxes. The man on the donkey can raise the dead.'

'The man's a blasphemer,' said Caiaphas, somewhat crestfallen.

'How can anyone blaspheme against a God that doesn't exist?' sneered the Centurion. 'Religion with you lot is just a crummy racket, a licence to mint money and exploit the poor.'

Caiaphas was still searching for a reply when a sergeant-at-arms rushed up, breathless, and saluted the Centurion. 'Permission to speak, sir?'

'Get on with it, man,' he snapped irritably.

'The Nazarene has entered the Temple courtyard, sir, and is driving out the moneychangers.'

'Not before time,' said the Centurion with a grin. 'Good for him.'

'Now's your chance,' shouted Caiaphas. 'Do your duty, arrest him. He's disturbing the peace!'

'And so are you. Cool it,' said the Centurion.

'Shall I arrest the Nazarene, sir?' asked the sergeant.

'If I had my way we'd give him a bloody medal,' replied the Centurion. 'No, you will not arrest him, Sergeant. We don't interfere in Temple business. Anyway, they have their own security force. But keep an eye on things and if there is a serious disturbance crush it without mercy and pull in the Nazarene if you have to. Dismissed!'

And as the soldier saluted and hurried away, the Centurion turned to Caiaphas. 'And you'd better bugger off and put your own house in order while you still have a roof over your heads.'

And with a brief nod to his boys to follow, Caiaphas buzzed off leaving the Centurion to ruminate alone. His eyes wandered Heavenwards and began to sparkle as he gave a devilish smile.

To Mike and Gaby, still glued to the monitor, he seemed to be smiling right at them. But it was probably just coincidence. Or was it? The Robots wondered.

'I'm confused,' said Gaby. 'Just whose side is this joker on?'

'Could be we've got him all wrong,' confessed Mike. 'Satan could be an invisible force.'

'But we've seen him,' protested Gaby. 'Remember that creepy little insect?'

'That could have been about as real as our Celestial City,' said Mike.

'You mean that all we saw was a hologram,' said Gaby. Mike nodded.

'So he could be anything,' said Gaby. 'A stone, a stick, a dog, or even a scrap of camel dung.'

'Or just a fly on the wall,' said Mike, swatting a blue-bottle. 'Anyway, it'll keep. Better be getting over to the Temple, I smell trouble.'

'Check,' said Gaby, touching a button.

And sure enough, in the Temple courtyard a near riot is in progress as Jesus overturns the tables of the money-changers and sends the coins spinning in all directions. Sacrificial doves flutter in the air and goats and sheep scatter as Jesus releases them. The Temple police try to retain order but are no match for the disciples who keep them at bay without inflicting any serious GBH. And in all this the goodies are cheered on by the thousand milling followers and citizens who have managed to crowd into the Temple courtyard. But things start to calm down after Jesus sweeps a smouldering sheep from a sacrificial altar before leaping up on to it to address the seething marketeers and moneychangers.

'The House of God should be a house of prayer but you have turned it into a circus.'

'And you have turned it into a madhouse,' screams Caiaphas in response as he arrives on the scene with the Mob.

'And you have turned it into a den of thieves,' responds Jesus, angrily pointing the finger of scorn. 'You forbid the people to bring their own beasts for sacrifice and force them to buy livestock from you at inflated prices. And they are only permitted to use Temple money which you sell them at a crippling exchange rate. You preach truth but practise corruption. You levy a Temple tax on the poor to keep you in luxury and snatch

the roofs from over the heads of widows unable to pay
and leave them to beg outside the Temple doors. And
I'm telling you, a time will come when your evil Temple
will come crashing to the ground in ruins with not one
stone left standing on another.'

SILENCE . . . for a moment . . . profound silence . . . as
if the world is holding its breath . . . Then a cacophony of
sound as everyone tries to get at Jesus. Most of them
want to raise him shoulder high in adulation, while
Caiaphas and his cronies would like to trample him
underfoot. But, strange to tell, nothing happens. It's as if
everyone is held by an unseen force – everyone, that is,
except Jesus, who turns and walks towards the archway
where M.M. and Lazarus are waiting for him. A moment
later Peter and the disciples follow him out into the street
where they are all swallowed up in the rush-hour traffic.

Suddenly the spell is broken as everyone in the courtyard blows their top and goes berserk.

'I think, if he'd given the word, they'd have torn the
Temple apart there and then,' said Gaby.

'Either that or the Mafia Mob would have torn *him*
apart,' said Mike. 'This is getting serious.'

'You mean it's getting out of hand,' said Gaby.

'We never programmed him to preach insurrection,'
said a worried Mike. 'It looks like our peace movement's
going up in smoke. What's got into him?'

'I'd say a little bit of Satan,' said Gaby, 'or maybe our
"Messiah" is just developing a mind of his own.'

'Makes you want to press the red button and blow
them all away,' said Mike despondently.

'And run the risk of Rossum blowing us away,' said Gaby. 'I don't know about you, Mike, but I feel we're reaching crisis point. Let's hang in there a while longer. Maybe that outburst was just a blip.'

'Bullshit,' said Mike, stepping out of character. 'It's all going down the tubes and you know it.'

Gaby was saddened by this sudden flash of pessimism and chose her words carefully before saying, 'Faith, Mike, we gotta keep our finger firmly on the faith button.'

Now it was Mike's turn to be phased by his partner's uncharacteristic utterance. There *was* no faith button, but he knew what she meant.

CHAPTER XIX

No Picnic!

et's check out the scene,' said Gaby, breaking the awkward silence that followed. 'Why don't I see what the Godfather's up to while you keep an eye on Jesus and the boys.'

Thankful for her initiative, Mike nodded and tuned into Jesus and his party while Gaby tracked down Caiaphas and the Mob.

They were tucked away in a top-security conference room deep in the heart of the Temple. The room had no windows and was lit only by the pale glow of oil lamps which threw menacing shadows on the faces of the hoods seated around a coffin-shaped table, trying to hide the fear that their days of racketeering were numbered . . . unless they got rid of Jesus.

Caiaphas, seated at the head of the table, puffed on his hubble-bubble pipe and glowered at his fellow priests, waiting for someone to get smart. It was uncanny, his resemblance to Sinatra.

'C'mon, Benny,' he growled at his chief henchman, who was sitting on his right. 'Gimme a lead.'

But Benny, who was the spitting image of Peter Lawford, was high on hashish and slurred, 'Why don't we send him for a swim in a pair of cement sandals?'

Whereupon Caiaphas blew a cloud of smoke in Benny's face, which induced a coughing fit, then turned to the hood on his left, who could have doubled for Dean Martin.

'So, Mac, what d'ya say?' Mac, who was handy with a knife, had nothing to say at all . . . so he got the smoke-in-the-face treatment too and likewise started to cough. And so it was left to that Sammy Davis Junior look-alike, Ezekiel (who was still out of favour regarding the Lazarus incident), to break the ice.

'Maybe we should get the Temple security guards to run him in, boss?'

'And be torn apart by the crowd. Are you crazy?' snarled the Godfather.

'I reckon the Romans would back us up, boss,' replied Ezekiel. 'They crack down real heavy on rioters.'

'Yeah, and guess who they'd indict? Have you ever seen the inside of a Roman jail?'

'No, boss,' he replied.

'Neither have I,' said Caiaphas. 'And I've no desire so to do. Don't kid yourself about the Romans – to them we're just one big pain in the ass. To them, the only good Jew is a dead Jew – and in the case of Jesus they got my vote.'

'Then, like I said, we gotta rub him out, boss,' coughed Benny.

'And fast,' coughed Mac. 'Didn't that cocksucker say before witnesses he'd blow away the Temple – that's insurrection. In my book we'd be poifectly within our rights to bring him to trial.'

'We have no rights,' said Caiaphas. 'The Temple stands because Rome chooses to let it stand. If Christ razed it to the ground tomorrow he'd be doing them a favour, believe me.'

'Aren't we overreacting, boss?' asked another sleazy member of the Mob. 'This guy's fulla hot air, and hot air never brought down pussy.'

'Right on,' said Ezekiel. 'What's the big deal, ain't no motherfucker born's gonna waste no goddamn Temple, not never, nohow.'

'Unless,' said Caiaphas, with only a hint of irony, 'he really is the son of God.'

'Don't tempt me, you scumbag,' muttered Gaby. 'All I have to do is raise my little finger to bury the lot of you. How's about it, Mike?' she said brightly to her partner, looking over her shoulder.

'Someday,' said Mike. 'But now is not the hour.'

'Spoilsport,' chided Gaby. 'So what's the Messiah doing, any more miracles coming up?'

'I thought I might need one when he went grocery shopping but he never had to put his hand in his pocket, not once – it was freebies all the way.'

'Seems that line of his is catching on,' said Gaby.

'What line?' queried Mike.

'You know – it's better to give than to receive,' said Gaby with a smile.

'I wouldn't bank on it,' said Mike, who was still a bit down in the dumps.

'Mike, your batteries need recharging,' said Gaby, and not for the first time. 'Nothing's happening that I can't handle – look, they're just schlepping up a hill heading for a picnic area.'

'Well,' said Mike with some reluctance (but not much), 'a brief shut-down might give me a fresh perspective on things.'

'Indubitably,' said Gaby, causing Mike to do a double take.

'And you'd reactivate me at the first sign of trouble?' asked Mike.

'Trust me,' said Gaby with the straightest of faces.

'Right then, I'll take forty winks,' said Mike, setting a dial on his belly button and giving it a push. *Click!* He was out of it.

Gaby shook her head, sighed with relief and relaxed. The strain was beginning to show. Rossum's Universal Robots weren't meant for this sort of emotional strain. They weren't programmed for it. It wasn't in their systems. They were currently functioning above the threshold of their output potential. Gaby felt like shutting down herself but they were reaching a crucial stage in their assignment – one of them had to be switched on twenty-four hours a day with their finger constantly on the button. She glanced at the monitor where Jesus and the disciples had just selected a shady spot under some olive trees and were settling down for their picnic. What the hell; nothing was going to happen for a while. So she put her feet up, switched on the TV and settled back to enjoy a Saturnine sit-com.

Back at the picnic it was all small talk – to start with. Gaby wasn't missing much. They were talking about the Temple, speculating on what it was like inside, for don't forget, they'd only got as far as the courtyard.

'They say the floors are paved with precious stones,' said Thaddeus.

'The crippled feet of the poor hobble over riches that would feed them and their families for the rest of their lives,' said Judas, pompously munching on a melon.

'They say it holds five thousand worshippers,' said Bartholomew.

'Go on,' said doubting Thomas with a grin.

'Ten thousand, I heard,' said Andrew expansively.

'Well, however many it holds there'll be thousands more at the door when the Master starts to preach there,' predicted Matthew.

'Then I'll be able to see for myself,' said Thomas.

'I wouldn't count on it, brother,' said Judas.

'What d'you mean?' piped up Mary Magdalene. 'Surely Jesus is gonna preach there?'

'What! In the ruins? You heard what the man said.' Judas turned to Jesus. 'That stupid broad seems hard of hearing, Master. Did you or did you not say you'd destroy the Temple and would not leave one stone standing on another?'

Before Jesus could reply Peter butted in. 'But that's just your way of speaking, isn't it, Master?'

Jesus said nothing, so Judas, misreading his silence for affirmation, stormed right on. 'And if that creep Caiaphas tries anything on, he'll have me to reckon with.'

'Frightening,' said M.M. sarcastically, still smarting from his last insult.

'Look, lady, we're talking men's talk here,' replied Judas condescendingly.

'And I'm talking the Master's talk,' said M.M., coming right back.

'Oh, and what's that, sister?'

'Jesus preaches peace, not punch-ups, brother,' she replied pointedly.

'Women hear only what they want to,' said Judas patronisingly. 'Your trouble is you don't think like a man.'

'But I know exactly how a man thinks,' she said with a smile.

Laughter from the others caused Judas to lose face and cool it, while M.M. took control.

'So tell us, Master, what's the next move? What happened today was beyond belief. Is there more to come?'

'Much more, Mary,' said Jesus softly. 'Much more.'

'We'll take Jerusalem by storm,' said Peter, on a high.

'Well said, boyo,' said Judas, backing him up. 'We're talking war here, isn't that so, Jesus?'

Jesus didn't reply straight off and when he finally did so his words came as a surprise to them all.

'You will hear of wars and rumours of wars, and the Temple will be destroyed . . . But not yet . . . And nation shall rise up against nation and there will be famine and desolation and disease . . . And this will be the beginning of sorrow . . . And you will be hated and persecuted for my sake, and the false prophets shall blacken the sky like vultures, and the light of the sun will be eclipsed by darkness and even love itself will grow cold . . . But those of you who hold fast to the truth and fed me when I was hungry, and took me in when I was naked, and comforted me when I was in prison, then you shall be saved; for whatever you do for others you do also for me, and the Kingdom of Heaven awaits you.'

No one spoke; the disciples were in shock – a state that became more profound as Jesus spoke again. 'Tonight we shall eat together for the last time. Go back into the city to the place that Mary and Lazarus have found for us. I will join you after dark for supper. Now go in peace,' said Jesus before they could put into words the thoughts buzzing around in their heads.

So, led by Mary, the disciples quietly departed, leaving Jesus resting against a gnarled old olive tree, deep in meditation.

And if Gaby had changed channels in time for the Master's prophecy things wouldn't have been too bad; she'd have been a little puzzled, it's true, for in her terms he was growing increasingly eccentric even though peace was still top of his agenda. As for all this

eternal life bullshit . . . ! Gaby shook her head at the
credulity of the man. But if it worked as a pacifier for
the masses, all well and good. Though why anyone
should hanker after anything as boring as life eternal
puzzled her profoundly.

CHAPTER XX

Scum in
a Turkish Bath

nyway, she *didn't* switch channel and was now hooked on a new programme – for the Saturnine sit-com had given way to an inter-galactic game show in which she found herself taking part. And the prize was a luxury holiday for two in the black hole of your choice. What a surprise that would be for Mike if she won. What a great time they'd have together. She was well ahead on points from her closest competitor, a Ti2E from TiTi2 3/4. Then her guilty-conscience circuit clicked in. Heck, this was supposed to be a weekend break! Why spoil it now

when she was feeling so much better already? OK, she'd take a quick peep down below just to be on the safe side . . .

Bzzz! It was just as she'd thought. There was the Messiah all alone in the olive grove enjoying a quiet siesta with no one to bother him. Even the blue-ass flies were giving him a break.

Click! And it was back to the game show with a clear conscience.

But things would have been different if she'd checked out Judas. Alarm bells would have been ringing and Mike would have been spinning like a top. And why? Because Judas was in conference with the Godfather. The location was a very select Turkish bath to which the errant disciple had been admitted only after pro- longed negotiations. Caiaphas was lying on a marble slab, sipping a Bloody Mary and getting a rub down from a blonde masseuse, while Judas hovered nearby fully dressed with his grimy garments getting wetter by the second. And, true to his word, Judas was about to make Caiaphas an offer he couldn't refuse.

'You want Jesus of Nazareth. I can deliver him,' said Judas.

'What's your price?' asked Caiaphas without cere- mony. 'What do you want in exchange?'

'Not what, boss, *who*,' replied Judas, licking the sweat from his upper lip. Both men sized each other up. Caiaphas decided to play it cool.

'Don't tell me you've got your eye on one of those Temple virgins,' he said with a leer.

'No, boss,' said Judas, leering back. 'I've got my eyes on stronger meat.'

'Oh, who exactly?' asked Caiaphas, losing his smile in anticipation of the reply.

'Barabbas,' said Judas, his eyes glowing fanatically.

'Are you out of your skull?' exploded Caiaphas. 'The Romans have him locked up in a top-security jail. They'd never release him, not even for me.'

'You're forgetting the Passover, boss, the amnesty! The one day in the year when those Roman bastards allow us the vote, the one day we can fool ourselves into thinking we have a say in our own affairs and vote for one lucky jailbird to be set free from his cage.'

'All right,' said Caiaphas after some consideration. 'Let's assume for a minute you can deliver, and this fake Messiah is tried for blasphemy and condemned to death, do you really believe the public would demand the release of that bum Barabbas instead of Jesus H. Christ?'

'If I can infiltrate the crowd with enough Barabbas supporters they will,' said Judas reassuringly. 'Especially if I can pass a little silver around to guarantee their enthusiasm.'

'And what do I get out of it?' growled Caiaphas. 'They both spell trouble. You heard Jesus say he'd destroy the Temple.'

'Jesus is full of shit,' sneered Judas. 'The only thing he's going to destroy is himself. He's a wanker.'

'Go for it,' said Caiaphas to the masseuse before resuming with Judas. 'If I had my way I'd lock 'em both up and throw away the key. It's just a matter of choosing the lesser of two evils.'

'Take your pick,' said Judas. 'Barabbas is only out to get the Romans. Jesus is after you lot – your money, your power, everything you've got!'

'And how do we pick the sucker up without starting a major riot?' demanded Caiaphas.

'That's my problem,' grinned Judas. 'Do we have a deal?'

'*Yeasoohyeahman*,' screamed Caiaphas as the blonde masseuse brought him to climax.

CHAPTER XXI

The Last Cuppa

aby lost out. The prize finally went to a 'Figment of the Imagination'. So she was not in the best of moods when she tracked Jesus down to an upstairs room in old Jerusalem where he was drinking tea and enjoying an aromatherapy foot massage at the hands of Mary Magdalene. A party was in progress with most of the disciples pissed out of their minds. Everything seemed OK. Thank Rossum she hadn't been needed – the 'guilty' light on her conscience circuit that had intermittently flickered on now flickered off for good. Yet something began to bother her . . . someone was missing.

★

By the time she realised that it was Judas, he was already coming through the door, balancing a heavy pitcher of wine on his shoulder. At the prospect of a refill the disciples held up their goblets and gave Judas a cheer. Only Jesus and M.M. remained sanguine, and it was to her that Judas turned his attention when he finally got around to giving her a refill.

'That wouldn't be oil of nard you're rubbing on the Master's feet, would it?' he said accusingly.

'The best,' said M.M. nonchalantly. 'Imported all the way from the Himalayas. I've been hoarding it for years, and never once broke the seal.' And she carefully poured a few more drops of the precious liquid into the palm of her hand.

Judas exploded. 'You're holding a small fortune there, woman, more than a working man earns in a whole year! You should have flogged it and given the money to the poor.'

'Lay off her, Judas,' said Jesus firmly. 'It's been a long day. The poor will always be with us, but my days are numbered. Mary is anointing me for my burial.'

Time seemed to miss a beat as the significance of his words struck home to everyone, including Gaby . . . But Jesus just continued calmly, 'And when my story is told to future generations Mary will be remembered for her kindness to me in my hour of need.' He swapped his teacup for a goblet of wine and proposed a toast. 'To Mary.'

With varying degrees of enthusiasm the disciples echoed the Master's words and drained their goblets, while M.M. herself looked as if she'd just won the lottery.

★

Then, as Jesus unexpectedly took up a loaf of bread and started to break it, the ship's transmitter went on the blink and vision and sound gave way to static and white noise.

'Shit,' snapped Gaby, beginning to panic. What to do? Try and re-establish contact or wake Mike? She glanced at the winkometer on his belly button, still nineteen winks to go before his wake-up call . . . unless she pressed it now! What would he think? He'd think she'd screwed up, that's what!! Then he'd be at panic stations too. Forget it. First, she'd try and sort it out herself.

But she was still feverishly checking circuits when, for no particular reason, normal transmission was resumed. Little seemed to have happened during the break – the disciples were still at the bottle. 'Boozy lot,' said Gaby to herself, wiping the sweat from her brow.

They are down to the very last goblet, passing it from lip to lip together with the kiss of peace that accompanies it. Last in the circle is Judas who drains the cup and looks at Jesus with loving but troubled eyes as he delivers his penultimate kiss.

'Lord, we gotta split the scene,' he whispers urgently. 'The Mob are casing the city joint by joint. There's a cave in the Garden of Gethsemene where we can hang out for the night and plan for tomorrow.'

'So be it,' says Jesus, staring him in the eyes unblinkingly.

'How considerate of him,' said Gaby to herself. Wrong, of course, but then she didn't know what we know. She didn't know that Judas had sold the Messiah down the river and nor did she know about the bread and wine. And there we also have the advantage on her – because we read all about it long ago at Sunday School. The bit where Jesus tore apart a loaf of bread and said to the disciples, 'Take this and eat, for this is my body.' And after taking a sip of wine he passed the goblet around for all to imbibe. 'No, this is not a wine tasting,' came Jesus' reply to Thomas' jokey question (he was *really* pissed), 'this is my blood which is shed for you and for many others to wash away your sins and bring you peace.' Gaby would have thought that Jesus had finally flipped! Either that, or Satan was playing some obscure game of his own. 'I mean, we're talking cannibalism here!' Isn't that what she would have thought?

It took them over an hour to reach the cave in the moonlit Garden of Gethsemene, and by that time most of the disciples were ready for a good kip. And once again Gaby considered waking Mike, but as he had only seven more winks to go it hardly seemed worth it, especially as things looked all set for a quiet night. So she continued her lone vigil and flicked in the infra-red system for a crisper view of events at the cave mouth.

'Rest here and sleep it off,' said Jesus to the weary disciples. 'I need to speak with my father.'

'I'll come with you, Lord, and keep watch,' said Peter.

'And I'll stand guard here,' said Judas.

Then, as the disciples filed wearily into the cave and Judas seated himself on a rock, Jesus and Peter moved off down the garden . . . tracked by Gaby in close-up . . . clearly showing Peter's deep concern for his troubled Master.

'Fear not, Lord, I will never leave you,' said Peter, brandishing his sword. 'I am ready to protect you and fight to the death.'

'Before the first cock-crow at dawn you will have rejected me three times over,' said Jesus sorrowfully.

'Never, Master,' protested Peter vehemently. 'I'd lay down my life for you.'

'Just go,' said Jesus.

As if reeling from a blow Peter stumbled off into the darkness, dimly conscious of Jesus sinking to his knees. Only Gaby heard the beginning of his prayer; the others were too far off.

'Dad, I've blown it! That little bit of Heaven I tried to bring down to Earth never made it. And so the pain and suffering begins . . . '

Jesus, racked with agony, begins to shake and sweat blood. His voice is dry and rasping. ' . . . And I just don't know if I can take it . . . So if you can ease the load, that'd be great. But if not, that's cool, I can handle it.' Suddenly he cries, 'Don't leave me!'

A shadowy figure approaches.

'I promised you, Lord, that I would not,' shouts Peter, mistakenly. 'That's why you must come with me quickly. I saw a flash of light just now, as of moonlight on armour.' Christ turns to Peter, for the first time revealing his bloodstained face. Peter is aghast, but before he can react Judas appears and, jumping to the erroneous conclusion that Jesus has been attacked by Peter . . . floors him with a piledriver of a punch.

'Bastard!' Judas cries, taking Christ by the shoulders and swinging him around the better to see the wound in the moonlight. But there is no wound and with an explosive sigh of relief Judas embraces Jesus and kisses him passionately. A shrill whistle sounds, there are cries and shouting. A Temple guard rushes up to the embracing couple, brandishing a spear. Peter sways to his feet – *Splat!* and almost slices off the guard's ear. Screaming in pain the guard collapses and the two men break apart as Peter turns on a second attacker.

Simultaneously Gaby hits Mike's winkometer and reactivates him at max-energy level.

'What's up?' he, not unnaturally, enquired.

'The Messiah's in deep shit,' gasped Gaby, fearful of the wrath to come. 'He's surrounded by Temple guards. Shall I gave them a plasma blast?'

'No, the hallucinatory effects are too unpredictable,' said Mike on autothink.

'That's a risk we gotta take,' shouted Gaby. 'Chances are it won't affect Christ at all. As for the others . . .' *Schzzz!* She never completed the sentence – an enormous flash knocked them both out and sent the ship spiralling out of control.

Jesus watches it weaving across the sky like a crazy comet – till it plunges from sight beyond the horizon. The next moment he is conscious of a ring of spears advancing towards him. Of Judas and Peter there is no sign. Jesus turns to the officer in charge.

'Put away your spears, I shall go in peace.' And then

he kneels to the guard writhing in pain at his feet and covers the bleeding ear with his hand. When he removes it the ear is completely restored and all sign of injury gone. At the sight of the miracle the Temple guards fall back in wonderment. Trembling, the cured man kisses Christ's feet and cries with joy, 'The Messiah, he is the true Messiah!' The spears of the soldiers begin to waver until the officer of the guard reinforces discipline.

'He is a *false* Messiah and he is under arrest. The charge is blasphemy.'

At the same moment another guard runs up to report to his superior.

'The disciples have scarpered, sir. There's a fire in the cave but the place is empty.'

'Hah!' mocks the officer. 'So the King has been abandoned by his subjects as a sinking ship is deserted by rats. Handcuff him, quickly, Caiaphas is waiting.' And as his hands are roughly fastened behind his back, Jesus, for the first time in his life, feels himself to be the loneliest creature in the universe.

As for his disciples, they had scattered like frightened sheep – all except Mary Magdalene who had to be dragged away physically by John. Even Peter's courage had failed him when it came to the crunch and he was humbled into shadowing the little procession at a safe distance as it made its way to the Temple where Jesus was to be softened up and interrogated.

CHAPTER XXII

Sharon and Debby
Point the Finger

lose to despair, Peter watched impatiently as Jesus approached the dark monolithic edifice that squatted like a giant turtle in the moonlight. It looked as if it would last a thousand years. Could that frail man being swallowed up in its maw really bring about its destruction? Despite himself Peter doubted it. For a moment he considered rallying the disciples and mounting a rescue operation. Judas would back him up for sure. But where was Judas? Where were the rest of them? In hiding, he guessed. At least he was still in touch with the Master, and might be of assistance, even yet. An hour passed; the hint of a new dawn bled

into the sky. A crowd was gathering. The grapevine had been busy. Two streetwise teenagers, Debby and Sharon, eyed Peter with suspicion, eventually daring to confront him.

'You're one of 'em, ain't cha?' said Sharon.

'Sorry?' said Peter, covered in confusion.

'Yeah, you are,' said Debby. 'We saw you at the Lion Gate with 'im on the donkey.'

'You're mistaken, girl,' said Peter abruptly.

'You talk like 'im an' all,' said Sharon. 'What's 'e been up to then?'

'Search me,' said Peter.

'Then wot you doin' 'anging around 'ere at this time 'a nite?' demanded Debby.

'Couldn't sleep,' said Peter, 'came out for a walk. Saw the crowd and thought I'd hang about. Anyway, what are you two doing up at this hour?'

'None of your bloody business,' said Sharon.

''Er dad's a Temple guard,' said Debby defiantly.

At this moment the doors are thrown open and Jesus appears, surrounded by the Temple guards who jostle him along. His hands are still fastened behind his back and he wears a blindfold. His body is bruised and there are abrasions on his face. He's obviously had a good working over. Peter is appalled. Suddenly a vicious shove sends Jesus stumbling straight into Peter's arms. At the same time Sharon catches sight of her dad.

'Hey, Dad,' she shouts above the din, 'these two's mates.'

''Ere, why aren't you back 'ome in bed?' he shouts back.

'Honest, Dad, we saw 'em together at the Lion Gate.'

'Don't forget your message, love,' prompts Debby as Dad continues to look baffled.

'Oh and Mum says yer breakfast's on the stove,' Sharon remembers suddenly. 'Gran's poorly again. She's 'ad to go over.'

'That old bag'll be the death of me,' says Dad despondently.

'What's the trouble there?' shouts the captain of the guard, hurrying over.

'My kid says she's seen this man fraternising with the prisoner, sir.'

'Do you know this man?' demands the captain, looking Peter straight in the eye. Peter releases his hold on Jesus, steps back a pace and replies forcibly, 'I've never seen him before in my life.'

'He's a fucking liar, Dad,' protests Sharon.

'Let's move it,' shouts the officer. 'King Herod doesn't like to be kept waiting. And get rid of the brat. Now!'

'Bugger off 'ome, you,' says Dad, giving Sharon a clip around the ear that sets her howling – until she recognises another collaborator. 'She was there too,' she sobs, pointing at M.M., trying to keep a low profile. The guards turn to look and wait for her to deny it. She doesn't, on the contrary:

'Too true, I was. Anybody have a problem with that?' she challenges. 'As for that tub of lard,' she says, glancing at Peter, 'I've never set eyes on him. But this man . . .' She elbows Peter aside and without ceremony whips off the bloody blindfold and dabs the sweat and blood from Jesus' face ' . . . This man I'm proud to know.' The Messiah and

M.M. look at each other with great tenderness and love. Silence . . . as everyone marvels at her courage . . . Then the sound of a cock-crow, followed by a great hubbub as Mary is arrested and Jesus is marched off by the guard, followed by the ever growing crowd. Peter is left alone with the two kids who sit in the gutter. Debby breaks off from comforting the weeping Sharon to spare a kind word for Peter.

'Sorry, Mister, it seems you weren't one of his mates after all.'

Peter buries his head in his hands, wishing he had never been born.

As for Mike and Gaby . . . they're still out of it.

CHAPTER XXIII

The Little
Ball-Breaker

erod was not an early riser; neither
was his step-daughter Salome nor
his wife Herodias. But Herodias
need not concern us, she'd gone to
Rome for the Spring Collection.
Normally they'd still all be in bed at
6 a.m. – in whose bed need also not
concern us – but today they were still up, looking bleary-
eyed and hung over. The last guests from last night's
orgy were just leaving the palace as Jesus and his escort
arrived along with Caiaphas, reclining on a litter.
Tumbling off it, he wasted no time in bowing to Herod
and whispering in his Royal ear, during which time the
Centurion and a detachment of guards representing the

power of Rome also turned up. It promised to be quite a party.

Perched high on his golden throne, Herod gloated down on the bedraggled figure of Jesus, who stared right back at him, calm and dignified.

'At last, after all these years, we meet face to face,' says Herod. 'We nearly met at your birth, you know. I missed you by minutes.' Jesus does not reply. 'Come, come. I know you are Jesus,' says Herod coaxingly. 'And that you suffer delusions of grandeur, imagining that you are both the King of the Jews and a prophet who works miracles. Perhaps you'd like to perform a miracle for us now; we haven't seen a miracle since the head of John the Baptist detached itself from his body.' Here Herod and Salome exchange wicked grins as he continues to goad Jesus.

'Miraculously cast off your bonds and you shall go free, I promise.' Still no response from the Messiah. Herod's eyes harden.

'Blindfold him,' he commands, and when this has been done he tips Salome the wink, which she knowingly returns. As usual the precocious teenager is overdressed and oversexed, reminding us today of Jodie Foster in *Taxi Driver* – even down to the heavy wedge shoes, one of which is about to connect, with ball-breaking impact, with the Messiah's unprotected testicles. *CRUNCH!* Jesus groans in pain and crashes to the floor – taking it on the chin. Many of the onlookers suffer with him, including the Centurion, if his expression of concern is anything to go by. Not so Herod who gives a harsh laugh and says mockingly, 'There, Prophet, prophesy who did that.'

With difficulty Christ staggers to his feet, but says nothing.

'He is as dumb as he is modest,' says Herod, hiding his exasperation. 'We must help him. Cut him loose.' This is done. 'Here, take my sceptre, my crown and my robe,' commands Herod. Whereupon he thrusts his regalia on to Jesus, leads him to the throne and roughly seats him.

'Here, take my throne as well. Salome, down on your knees, crawl and kiss his feet. Pay homage to the King of the Jews.'

Exchanging another wink with Herod Salome obeys, and even goes one better, giving the Messiah's feet a sex-kitten kind of licking – culminating in a toe-sucking such as to bring a lesser man to orgasm. After which she then looks up at his blindfolded features and says earnestly, 'All my life I have sought you and at last I have found you, my Lord. Now let me hear it from your own lips, tell me you are the Messiah, tell me. Are you the son of God?'

'You seem to think so,' said Jesus simply.

'From your own lips, let me hear it.'

'Soon you will see the Son of Man sitting at the right hand of God, flying on the clouds of Heaven,' said Jesus.

This is the moment Caiaphas has been waiting for and as the treacherous Salome smiles triumphantly at Herod, the Godfather points his staff at Jesus and declaims in high dudgeon, 'There he stands, condemned from his own mouth. Blasphemy, self-confessed! You are guilty and must suffer death by the casting of stones. And . . . '

Herod interrupts, commandingly, 'No, he is not worthy of such a fate. This is no prophet but a common criminal guilty of rioting and sedition and as such must suffer the penalty prescribed by Caesar.' He turns to the Centurion. 'Escort this man to the Governor. He is guilty of crimes against the state and is answerable to the law of Rome.'

But the Centurion sees that despite his macho front Herod is really intimidated by Jesus and is afraid to pass the sentence of death himself. He just wants to pass the buck and the Centurion wants to block him.

'But the prisoner is from Galilee, your Majesty. That is your territory. It's not part of the Roman Empire. All its people are under your jurisdiction.'

'But his crimes are against Rome and warrant death by crucifixion, and under the terms of our treaty I am denied the right to pass such sentence. Take him to Pontius Pilate.'

The Centurion grits his teeth and gives the necessary orders. Herod has secured the death penalty without being directly involved. Herod has won.

But Mike and Gaby knew none of this.

CHAPTER XXIV

Rub-a-Dub Dub, Pilate's in the Tub

aiaphas was furious. Herod's intervention had complicated matters. He had to get to the Governor, Pontius Pilate, before the prisoner and escort in order to put his case. He could make the blasphemy charge stick all right, there were witnesses, but the charge of sedition might be harder to substantiate. However, although they were far from being best buddies Caiaphas had proved himself a useful collaborator and provided Pilate with many a fruitful tip-off, for which he received occasional favours in return, so he might well get lucky.

When Caiaphas arrived at the Governor's residence all hot and flustered and on foot – his litter had broken down when one of the bearers burst an artery – Pilate was in the bath with a couple of concubines. The Governor was not best pleased at this intrusion on his ablutions but, guessing the reason must be pretty damned important, reluctantly granted an audience.

In a few well-chosen words Caiaphas explained the situation and gave Pilate a quick briefing, so that by the time Jesus arrived in the company of the Centurion and two guards Pilate was well primed. By the way, he bore a striking resemblance to David Bowie in *The Last Temptation*. Not wishing to waste time on niceties, Pilate launched straight into the attack with his trick question – courtesy of Caiaphas.

'Tell me, do you think it fair and just that Jewish citizens should be burdened by our heavy Roman taxes, or not?'

Jesus, still suffering from his previous softening up, transcends his pain to answer coherently. 'Show me the money with which the taxes are paid.'

Pilate begins to regret his acquiescence to this 'informal' trial. 'This is absurd. Come along, Caiaphas, show him the colour of your money.'

Somewhat flustered by this unexpected turn of events Caiaphas produces a fat purse and pulls out a few Roman coins.

'Stop playing games,' he snaps as Jesus. 'You know the coins of the realm perfectly well.'

'With whose face are they stamped?' asks Jesus.

'With Caesar's, of course,' Caiaphas snaps back.

'Then give to Caesar the things that are Caesar's, and to God the things that are God's,' says Jesus.

Pilate laughs. 'He got you there, Caiaphas. What did you hope to prove?'

'That he is a revolutionary and a threat to the cause of Imperial Rome,' says Caiaphas forcefully.

'Is that right, Centurion?' asks Caesar.

The Centurion replies with some reluctance, 'True, he drove the moneychangers from the Temple, Excellency, but they've been ripping off the public for years. And he *did* threaten to destroy the Temple, as Caiaphas himself can testify.'

'He already has,' says Pilate, and a lot more besides. He looks at Jesus. 'Poor deluded man,' says Pilate. 'Another victim of the Jerusalem syndrome. The place is fairly crawling with Messiahs all in need of treatment. I find a dose of strong medicine usually effects a cure. Give him fifty lashes and send him on his way, Centurion.'

'But he has committed blasphemy and according to our laws must be executed,' butts in Caiaphas.

'And you want me to sign the death warrant?' says Pilate.

'We will naturally pay a tribute to Rome to cover the administration costs,' says Caiaphas unctuously.

Despite the promised bribe Pilate is in a bit of a pickle and hesitates. Of late he has been heavily censured by Rome for being too liberal with the death penalty and one more needless execution might be the last straw as far as his future is concerned. The Centurion knows this and comes to his rescue.

'If I might suggest, Excellency, today is the Feast of the Passover when the Governor has the authority to pardon a felon. You would be perfectly within your rights to release the prisoner.'

Pilate's face lights up as Caiaphas' darkens, until, coincidentally, a rhythmic chanting sounds from the street below.

'Barabbas, Barabbas, Barabbas.' The Centurion goes to the balcony to check it out. Sure enough, there is Judas leading the crowd and stirring them up as promised.

The Centurion turns to Pilate. 'It seems, Excellency, that the people are set on a pardon for Barabbas and, unfortunately, on this one day of the year the people have the last word.'

Now it is Pilate's turn to look angry and Caiaphas' turn to look pleased, although he does his best not to show it.

'Fuck it!' says Pilate before turning to Christ. 'Seems it's just not your day, Jesus.' Then he catches sight of the gloating Caiaphas and decides to piss on his parade. 'Centurion,' he commands, 'have a sign nailed to the cross proclaiming "Jesus of Nazareth – King of the Jews".'

Caiaphas' face clouds over. 'Might I suggest, Excellency – "This man *said* he was King of the Jews"?'

'And I want it written in three languages,' says Pilate, ignoring him. 'And that's an order.'

'Very good, Excellency,' says the Centurion, saluting.

'Now give him a good flogging for being such a pain in the ass and send him to Golgotha! Now get out, the lot of you – I wash my hands of the whole affair.'

And as they go, Pilate turns, business-like, to the more buxom of the two concubines and starts lathering her double-D bosoms while the other one wastes no time in going down beneath the bath water. Executions are such a big turn on.

CHAPTER XXV

Crucifixion Carnival

ike and Gaby were still in orbit when for no apparent reason their power was restored. One minute they were just a thousand tons of dead metal imprisoned in space, the next they were a hundred thousand throbbing circuits in action programming A.R.K. 2001's race back to Jerusalem. The Robots, who'd been reactivated at the same time, postponed thoughts of a post-mortem in the panic to get back to Jesus and shield him from harm.

Too late! By the time they locate him, Jesus is already nailed to the cross, getting an earful from Caiaphas, who is reclining comfortably on a litter surrounded by the Mob.

'Come on, Jesus of Nazareth,' he shouts. 'If you really are God Junior then get your old man to unhook you and make with the Band-Aids.'

The Mob crack up while the felon hanging on the cross to the left of Jesus also puts in his two cents' worth. 'Save us! If you are the son of God, save us, you son of a bitch.'

When the suffering Jesus manages to stammer a reply it is barely audible. 'For . . . give them, Dad, for . . . give them, they don't know shit from shinola.'

The crucified criminal hanging on Jesus' right also manages a few words. 'Hang in there, man, and when it's all over spare a thought for yours truly.'

'Sure thing, pal,' gasps Jesus. 'Tonight we'll have a ball . . . in Paradise.'

'It takes a bullshitter to know a bullshitter,' scoffs Caiaphas, to the delight of the Mob and members of the holiday crowd attracted by the free entertainment.

Meanwhile Mike and Gaby, having got their shock/ horror system under control, zap into supersonic-mode, or as near as makes no matter.

'We can withdraw the nails from his body with a high charge of e.m.f.,' gabbles Gaby, 'then teleport him straight back to the ship.'

'Where we can perform a few life-saving miracles of our own,' gushes Mike.

But as they rapidly set things in motion, Christ smiles compassionately down on the sad figure of Mary his

mother, who is praying for him, then lifts his eyes to
Heaven for the last time and says in a whisper, 'I'm on
my way, Da . . . ' And his head slumps forward as his
heart gives its last tortured beat – and the life goes out of
him. The 'options' circuits of the Robots race – but
come up with no solutions. They are further phased by
the actions of the Centurion who snatches a spear from
one of the soldiers and plunges it into Christ's right side.
Blood and water gush forth, whereupon the Centurion
leers straight into the Robots' lens and mocks contemptuously, '*This* was truly the son of *God*?'

And then as Mike and Gaby watch incredulously, the
Centurion screams with satanic laughter and begins
metamorphosing into the repulsive beetle-like creature
we recognise as Satan. Simultaneously the sky darkens
and the Earth starts to quake, snow falls, lightning
flashes and thunder roars. People drop to their knees in
terror. Caiaphas and the Mob run like hell and even
Satan, no longer laughing, scuttles madly for cover. The
snowstorm turns into a blizzard – followed by a bolt of
lightning which blows every circuit in the ship – *blackout*!

CHAPTER XXVI

The Big Bang

hat's the second time in forty-eight hours we've been zapped,' said Gaby, groping about in the emergency locker for a candle and a box of matches. Although, truth to tell, she was in no great hurry to strike a match. That would have meant a face-to-face confrontation with Mike, and then how would she be able to hide the guilt she felt at producing such an almighty fuck-up? Maybe she should activate her self-destruct button and get it over with, now! For any R.U.R. Court Martial would certainly pass the termination sentence after hearing her incriminating testimony regarding all the crimes and misdemeanours

of which she was guilty – all the way from malpractice to second-degree mutiny. She couldn't even give false evidence and get away with it – the lie detector built into her circuits would come into immediate operation – and result in instant meltdown. The very thought was suicidal. But what bothered her most of all was the realisation that she had let Mike down – badly! Worse than badly, catastrophically. After all, as captain he would have to carry the can for the débâcle. She was in such a state that she dropped the matches.

'What's that?' said Mike, startled by the sound.

'I dropped the matches,' said Gaby.

'For a moment I thought it was raining in here,' said Mike with a nervous laugh of relief. They both bent down in the dark to pick them up – and their fingers touched.

'Why, you're trembling like a leaf,' said Mike in amazement . . . and held her hand a little tighter.

'Mike, I screwed up,' said Gaby with a gush of emotion. 'I thought I could handle things. I guess I've got an ego problem.'

'There, there,' soothed Mike. 'Don't put yourself down. That's not the reason and you know it. The fact is that I'm soon for the big scrap heap in the sky. I wasn't built to be in a constant state of overdrive and you just wanted to give me time to cool down – Rossum bless you.'

Gaby's reply was a big sob followed by an exclamation of disbelief from Mike as a drop of warm H_2O hit his hand.

'Gaby, what's this? Robots don't cry.'

At this Gaby broke down completely and collapsed sobbing against Mike with a big, heartfelt *clunk!* Then, as he put his arms around her and gently patted her shoulder, Mike found his own eyes moistening too . . . and fought like mad to hold back the tears.

'Come on, you, you big hunk,' said Gaby, half laughing, half crying in the dark, 'now you're blubbing too.'

'No I'm not,' choked Mike, trying to maintain his manhood.

'You are, too,' said Gaby, breaking away to strike a light. And in the flare of the match they both marvelled at their incredible tear-stained faces.

'Do you know what?' said Gaby, gazing with loving eyes through the tears.

'What?' said Mike, brushing his own tears away.

'I'm beginning to believe in miracles.'

And as Mike beamed love back at her a wonderful thing came to pass . . . music filled the sphere, music of indescribable beauty which affected the Robots almost as if it were programming them. The match burnt out restoring the ship to darkness . . . but the otherworldly music rolled on accompanied by a succession of extraordinary sounds emanating from the Robots themselves – everything from tintinnabulation to trumpet tattoos and cybernetic cymbal clashes, to clinking castanets and cantatas on the cello, voluntaries on the violas and clarion calls on the clarinets, bacchanals on the basses, paroxysms on the piccolo and farting on the faggotti . . . all building to the whirlwind whine of a spin-dryer clunking out of control with an unbalanced load threatening to rock itself silly.

Simultaneously, the Robots began to glow, revealing what appeared to be a pulsating mobile metal puzzle. For where there had been two Robots there is now only one – as we realise with a deep, deep blush that Mike is riding Gaby – doggy style. *Wahoo-wahoo! Ding! Ding! Ding!* Whistles blow and bells clang as the Robots *C★L★I★M★A★X!!*

'YES!' the Robots scream in unison to the sound of orgasmic chords on the organ and groaning metal fatigue. The glow fades – discreetly returning the ship to darkness.

'That was great, Mike,' murmured Gaby after a while, 'but you can back up now, honey – time to wash off.' There followed the sound of escaping steam and two sighs of deep satisfaction.

Well, I suppose it had to happen sooner or later and Rossum in his wisdom had allowed for it. Having created the Animal Kingdom (so we are told) and a vastly superior breed of Robot he could hardly deny this metal master-race the one pleasure common to the very lowliest beast, so he'd gone one better and programmed music of the spheres into the act and a host of other goodies even beyond our ken. I tell you, if an animal, and yes, that includes you, dear reader, had ever experienced to even a hundredth degree what the Robot Race experienced at the '*Eternal Moment*' (as it is called) you'd think you'd died and gone to Heaven. And the fact that Mike and Gaby had waited a quarter of a million light years before dedicating themselves to the act showed in what high esteem it was held. And such was the potency of the act that it might be half a light year before the Robots felt ready to repeat the experience.

As for the gestation period, if pregnancy occurred, that varied, just as it does in nature. In a life form such as our own, which developed from a single cell in the warm Sargasso Sea, birth comes relatively fast after fertilisation, but as we know all too well such unselective reproduction is susceptible to any number of fatal defects resulting in a species of disease-ridden organisms, doomed to die from the instant of conception. Not so Rossum's Universal Robots.

But I digress. This is not a commercial for Rossum who, despite his genius, was still struggling after aeons of research to find an antidote to the creeping peril that threatened to ultimately destroy his universe. Yes, RUST – the four-letter word that struck fear into the tin hearts of every single one of the two million metal men, women and children that gyrated around the five corners of his galaxy. And time was running out – their days were numbered; a fact well worth reiterating, and then some.

CHAPTER XXVII

Oops!

alf a million years and what scientific advances of real worth had mankind achieved? The wheel, the pyramid and the condom (manufactured from a camel's bladder), their main efforts having so far been channelled into the invention of weapons of mass destruction like boiling lead and the long-range catapult. The hopes of Mike and Gaby for world peace and the discovery of a rust-proof paint lay buried in a rocky hillside on the outskirts of Jerusalem. They would have to abort their noble experiment and start again. They had the will – reinforced by rejuvenating *supersex*; now all they needed was a fresh opportunity.

But first they had to pick up the body for the post-mortem which was standard practice with every indoctrinated new species.

Teleportation was the obvious choice but the unit had been knocked out of commission when the ship took the hit from the thunderbolt that sent it off course. There was nothing for it – they'd have to disembark. It was like leaving the womb – a vulnerable journey into the unknown. Still, needs must. So with the ship, still invisible to the naked eye, hovering a hundred feet above terra firma they stepped into space and sped towards Christ's tomb – a stone's throw from Golgotha. It was dawn and nobody was hanging about . . . except for the familiar figure of Judas who was suspended from a withered tree on the hillside by a rope around his neck. Shocked and surprised, the Robots hovered in for a closer look.

'D'you suppose it was guilt?' asked Gaby.

'Maybe,' said Mike, 'or maybe it was the Mafia.'

'What's that?' queried Gaby, pointing at something glinting in the early morning light beneath Judas' turban.

'Let's have a look-see,' said Mike, and kicked the turban off – to reveal thirty silver electrodes embedded in the dead man's skull.

Then it hit them! Judas was a cyborg . . . of course! It made perfect sense. With Satan taking on the form of the Centurion, Judas was the perfect spy satellite in the cold war between the rival scientists. A war the Robots had seemingly lost.

'Let's get out of here,' urged Gaby. 'I'm spooked.' And with the speed of Puck she quit the scene and a second

later was hovering above the tomb with Mike only a beat
behind her. Three humans looked up at them with open
mouths – the two Temple guards who had been posted
to arrest Jesus, in case he kept his word and rose from the
dead, and M.M. who had been released from custody
and was keeping a prayerful vigil. They could hardly
believe their eyes; no, they didn't see the two technological metal marvels levitating before them, but two
holograms of the Archangels Michael and Gabriel as
visualised in High Renaissance art. Two blasts of CO_2
(laughing gas) and they were laughing themselves to
sleep.

Next the Robots were confronted by an almighty
boulder blocking the mouth of the cave, which Mike
reduced to atoms in less than a moment. With some
trepidation they entered the cave and came to a stand-
still. There, lying in a simple robe on a rose-coloured
slab of stone, was the frail figure of Jesus. He had been
bathed and anointed and looked a million dollars. And as
two pairs of eyes set in two tons of metal registered the
fact that he was good and dead, two lumps rose in their
respective throats and water trickled from their optical
cavities. They had known him, man and boy, for thirty-
three years and never missed a birthday. They had heard
his first words 'Gaby' and 'Mike' – (though his mother,
bless her, had always thought he was talking gobbledy-
gook). They had both been present at his circumcision,
watched him take his first steps, nursed him through
mumps and whooping cough, removed the first
gafilterfish-bone from his throat, helped him fly his
first kite, set him up on his first date, videoed his bar

mitzvah and God knows what else. They both knew they shouldn't be feeling this way, it wasn't in their specifications, but, then again, Rossum moves in strange ways.

'If only we could resurrect him like Satan raised Lazarus,' said Gaby, shedding more tears.

'We've a long way to go before we achieve that kind of technology,' said Mike, stifling a sob. 'Satan's light years ahead of us there.'

'Someone mention my name,' said Satan, suddenly materialising.

Gaby nearly threw up at the sight of his bulbous beetle-like body but Mike managed to keep his nausea in check and tried to act as if he was having a perfectly civilised conversation with a fellow Robot, but one of an inferior class.

'Top of the mornin' to yez, me boyo. What brings yerself here on this cold and frosty Easter Saturday?'

For an answer the beetle farted (he was a mutated descendant of the dung beetle) and said in a fair imitation of Noël Coward, 'Partaking of an early breakfast, dear boy – camel droppings are at their very best at sun-up. And like yourselves I felt I should pay my last respects to an old friend.'

'After making sure he was good and dead,' snapped Gaby, beginning to lose it. 'And why did you fuck up our experiment?'

'Because, dear lady,' replied the beetle patiently and politely, 'you were throwing good money after bad. The fulfilment of the laws of harmony should be our topmost ambition, I quite agree. Your aims were laudable but your basic material was irretrievably flawed. But instead of scrapping it and starting afresh, as every good truth-seeker should, you attempted to fix it by feeding it a tissue of false information. This is contrary to the laws of logic that govern the universe, and as a moral guardian of these laws it is my duty to administer fair play.'

The Robots were at a total loss. Suddenly *they* were the ones that were in the wrong. All their concern for Christ and the way and the truth were based on ulterior motives with the end justifying the means.

'I won't question your motives,' said Satan, almost reading their thought patterns. 'I'm sure they are laudable enough, even if hopelessly misguided, but don't you see, my dear chaps, you would *never* have got your sad little human creatures to return to their original natures; never in a million years. They had their chance and they crucified it. I intervened because you were cheating, what with all your miracles and what not. It's simply not cricket.'

'But why all the fun and games and fancy dress?' said Gaby.

'Even since childhood I've had an absolute passion for charades,' replied Satan with a devilish wink . . . and then, becoming serious, 'I should take care of that right away if I were you; you are both developing early signs of rust around your eye sockets.'

Mike and Gaby exchanged fearful glances. What he said was true.

'Silly of me,' smiled Satan, 'I'm sure that anyone who can raise the dead will have found an answer to that little problem absolute aeons ago.'

But the smile faded as soon as he got the drift of Mike's next question.

'You mean you can't, can't . . . ' Mike couldn't bring himself to say it, so Satan said it for him.

'Can't reactivate dead matter . . . ? No, that's way beyond our capabilities. As a matter of fact I was going to ask you for the formulae.'

'Well, if you weren't responsible for raising Lazarus from the dead, and we weren't responsible either,' mooted Gaby, 'who the fuck was?'

And right on cue, with a barely audible chuckle, Jesus dematerialised.

Rossum Gratias